Her New Cuckold: The First Chapters

by KinkyWriter

Contents

Her New Cuckold
...Locked

Her New Cuckold … Locked

"

I really do think that it's time you put him into chastity, Kate," Marcus told her as the two dined in the private section of the iconic restaurant that featured panoramic views of the city. "He'll be much more compliant and less likely to question what you do with me if you do…"

"I suppose…" the woman sighed as she took another sip from her wine glass. "I was just hoping that it wouldn't have to come to that … that he'd just learn to accept what I want on his own."

Her date smiled his award-winning smile from across the

table, then comforted her, "Men aren't quite that easy, my dear. You've been married to him for 15 years now – it's no surprise that he would provide a little *resistance* when coming to learn that his loving wife wants to start dating again."

"But it's nothing against *him,* per say," she protested to no one in particular, "I just want … *more!*"

"And you *deserve* more!" Marcus implored back. "I think you've taken marvelous strides these last couple of months indulging with me, though we haven't had nearly as many *work outings* as I would like to give you the excuses that you require to get out of the house. He already has a suspicion that you have *ulterior motives* to your nights out – why not put your foot down and *remind him* who's the boss so that you can stop dancing around our time together and enjoy it all the more?"

"But I **do** *enjoy dancing with you!"* Kate purred back with a grin as she took a bite of the raspberry cheesecake between them.

Marcus smiled, *"You know what I mean!"*

The two laughed and enjoyed their view out the window that Marcus had been able to procure with his connections before Kate turned the conversation unexpectedly back to her husband's chastity, to her date's pleasure…

"I don't even know which one to get – I looked through that website that you gave me for an hour the other day and I have no idea what I'm looking at!"

"Well, why didn't you just say so?!" Marcus grinned as he reached down into the bag at his feet as he pulled out his iPad, then slid his chair around next to his date's so that they could both see the screen at the same time. Pulling up the same website that he had given the woman to browse earlier, he began to give Kate a basic tutorial of chastity belts and the different types that the site sold and how they all worked…

"There are two basic types of devices used for male chastity," the handsome man explained, pointing to the pictures on the tablet that he held between them. "There are cages, and there are belts, and they're both designed pretty much like they sound…"

"Cages, on one hand, are typically something that locks

behind the cock and balls, and then protrudes down to cover either one or both to prevent access to the genitals by the wearer. Some of the most common, inexpensive ones for beginners are made of plastic, *like these,* and in theory prevent the wearer from becoming hard enough to ejaculate."

"Well he's a beginner," Kate replied curiously, *"so I should get him one of these? That doesn't look too bad for $150…"*

Marcus smiled and held up a hand before reaching his arm around her, "I *did* say *'in theory'* … because it's been said that some men have still been able to bring themselves to orgasm in these things given enough time and enough stimulation, and if push comes to shove, *plastic* isn't exactly the most unbreakable substance on Earth!"

"So then maybe we go with one of these metal cages – *they look pretty fierce!"* she joked as she slid her finger across the tablet to move the site to the next page.

"Oh, they are!" her friend concurred. "You can see here that when you move up to steel, there are a whole lot more options with what you can do – they have cages that cover the entire cock and balls together, they have special devices that require *a piercing through the penis* to be locked in place … *for additional security,* and they even have devices that contain sharp spikes like these on the inside," he pointed out in one of the more menacing devices after zooming in on the screen to show their detail.

"Ouch! Wouldn't that be … *painful???*" Kate asked with a wincing look on her face.

"Yes," he confirmed with a warm smile. "If someone were, to say, *become aroused at the thought of his wife being out with another man,* the spikes inside of a chastity cage like that would be *very painful* for him…"

"I see…" she purred as a small grin slipped across her face as she looked back at her date and winked.

"Now there are also chastity *belts,* which are more along the lines of the traditional sense that you would expect," he continued, "where there's actually *a belt* that locks around the wearer's waist, with a separate device that loops between the legs to prevent access to the genitals themselves…"

"So what's the difference?" Kate asked curiously as she scanned the new array of devices that appeared on the screen.

"Well, for one – *security*," he stated. "One could argue that some of the metal cages, *especially those that involved piercings,* are fairly secure and inescapable, however the way most belts are designed, instead of simply attacking the piece around the genitals themselves, you'd actually have to remove the belt as well, which is typically made of a very high-grade steel that would be quite difficult, *not to mention dangerous,* to cut while still locked around the body."

"Additionally, there's the question of *thoroughness* because as you can see here, with *these belts* the entire cock and balls are *hidden away* from the outside world as well as from everyday contact with the wearer himself. It's been said that they're quite *intimidating* due to how they put the wearer in a position where he can no longer touch or even see his own cock anymore…"

Kate raised her brow in curious contemplation.

"So how long would he be able to wear something like this??? Would he be able to last the entire evening while we go out, or would it need to be a short night so that I could let him out to pee?"

Marcus grinned as he flipped through the remaining pictures on the site.

"Actually, even the simplest of cages like we looked at earlier are made to be worn for *days or weeks* at a time, and it's not entirely unheard of for people who are really into male chastity to keep their submissives caged for *months on end,* some even *permanently…*"

Kate's eyes grew wide.

"Of course," he added, "for extended durations, he'd need to be released every now and then for *more thorough cleaning* and whatnot…"

"But he could use the bathroom in one of these … *even the belts???*" she inquired with astonishment as she reached again for her glass of red wine, now thoroughly intrigued by her friend's show and tell.

"Oh yes," he replied with a pearly white smile. "For all of them, the wearer can easily still urinate out the end, although he'll definitely be limited to *sitting down* to avoid making a mess. It will also take a bit of extra time afterwards to *clean up,* but that's very minor considering the benefits of chastity…"

"As for #2, well, *obviously* the cages pose no real problem because they're secured only to the cock and balls. The belts, on the other hand, are a bit more complicated and some care needs to be taken, however as you can see *here* — all of the belts that this site sells feature *a hole* in the back that aligns with the asshole for going to the bathroom."

"They even have a feature here," he added with a smirk, *"if you feel like* **getting kinky,** *where you can* **add a butt plug** *that locks into the hole in the belt and is held in place as long as the chastity belt remains locked around his waist!"*

"Wow," Kate laughed astonishingly as her eyes scanned back over the page again, focusing in on the aforementioned anal attachment.

Marcus laughed along with her as he handed her the tablet and allowed her to continue to browse on her own while he flagged the attention of their server to bring him a cup of coffee. He watched his beauty curiously browse through the various devices that he had just shown her, amused even as she stopped for a few seconds longer on the cage that featured the sharp spikes and laughed quietly to herself. Finally stopping back on the last page that they viewed that showcased the full-featured, steel belts, she sighed as she looked over the page, then up to the view out the window before asking, *"But what makes you think that he'll even go along with it???"*

The man turned in closer to the woman and stroked her long, brown hair gently as he explained, "Two reasons … **Number One,** because *I know men like your husband,* and men like your husband are *naturally submissive creatures.* It's the reason that he's sitting at home watching TV right now instead of *storming through this restaurant, threatening to* **punch my lights out.** He's gentle, and he's passive, and he's *perfect* for a strong woman like you because he gives you the freedom to go out and do the things in life that you want to do."

Kate softly smiled as she glanced over at him, setting the iPad on the table and taking his hand in hers, then asking, "And the second reason???"

"Because you're not going to give him any choice otherwise," Marcus told her smoothly before leaning in to suck her sweet, burgundy lips into his. The two kissed passionately in the dim corner of the restaurant for several seconds before

they broke and he whispered sensually to her, *"Isn't that how they tell me that* **marriage** *works — the wife tells the husband to do something, and the husband* **does it?!"**

"Something like that…" Kate purred as she slid into him for another kiss while she savored the doctor's firm embrace around her.

"But how am I supposed to get him to put it on?" she asked between breaths, trying but failing to be cautious of how intimate she should be with her secret lover in public.

"You don't even need to worry about that, my dear," he cooed as she melted in his lap. "We'll just order it and when it comes, I'll have one of the other nurses stop by your house after we go out to fit it on him."

Kate laughed as she rested her hand on his chest.

"Right, like he's really going to go for *just some random lady from my work showing up* **to lock him in chastity???"**

"Not *just some random lady,* he won't," he replied with a grin, "but I'd bet you he'd do it if *Veronica* showed up at his door!"

Kate's mind flashed to the sexy blonde she worked with who was about 10 years younger than she was and always seemed to turn heads, whether she was dressed up for a company function or even just wearing their everyday work attire…

"Mmmmm – ok, so maybe that might work…" she laughed as she stole another nibble from his lips before settling back into her own chair and taking another look at the options that were displayed up on the pad. Quietly flipping back and forth between several of the more encompassing belts that they had discussed, she paused as she zoomed into the prices on each, then turned back to Marcus with a frown.

"There's no way that I can afford one of these things, though," she sighed as she realized that the models she had most piqued an interest in were all over a thousand dollars each. "Even if it would be a lot of fun, I just couldn't do that to our budget…"

Marcus just grinned, to which she replied, "What?" before he laughed and explained to her, "I never had any intention of *you* having to pay for this! Which one do you like?"

She glanced over at him suspiciously, then turned her attention back to the iPad where she flipped back and forth between two models before finally selecting one that bore a price of nearly $1,400 plus taxes and shipping. Pointing to the device on the screen, Kate looked up at her date and curiously asked, "How about this one?"

He took the tablet from her and zoomed in to quickly read the description, then looked back at her with a wink and replied, "Nice choice! It will take about six weeks to get here once we order it, so you'll just need to figure out a way to get the measurements that we need without *spoiling* your little surprise…"

Kate felt a chill rush through her body as she considered what was being proposed, then leaned in to cuddle with Marcus as she asked him softly, "And you're sure it's not too much???"

Marcus reached over to pull the woman onto his lap as he stared into her deep, hazel eyes before bringing his tongue to meet inside of her mouth hungrily as she felt the passion stir underneath his pants.

"Look around you," he whispered to her seductively.

"Nothing's too expensive for my lover…"

"If that's the case," Kate purred back, *"can I get the one with the spikes in it, too?"*

"If that's what turns you on…" he told her with a chuckle as he nibbled at her lips.

"It just might!" Kate giggled in his lap. "You're turning me on to all sorts of new things lately…"

Marcus smiled as he kissed the woman openly and deeply, leaving her breathless as he proposed, "Then maybe we should take this over to the hotel room that I reserved for us across the street. They've got a bottle of champagne waiting for us on ice, and the room has a jacuzzi with a view that's even better than this one…"

"You know there's something that I'm interested in even more than the view!" Kate retorted playfully as she grabbed at the man's erection discretely.

"Well I've got plenty of *that* ready and waiting for you, too…"

The two savored each other's embrace for a minute longer

until Kate could feel herself getting wet between her thighs before glancing down at the time and regretfully protesting, "But you know that if I come over to the hotel, I'm going to end up spending the night and then I'll have to come up with some excuse to explain to Andrew why I was out all night again!"

"Why do you think that I got the room?!" Marcus replied without missing a beat.

"And besides," he added with a sly grin, *"just think - once that chastity belt arrives, you won't have to explain a thing anymore…"*

* * * * * * * * *

Andrew walked into the bedroom, finding his wife unexpectedly sitting at the vanity doing her makeup and asked, "So what are your plans for tonight?"

Without looking up as she steadied to apply her eyeliner, Kate replied, "Oh, I thought I told you – I'm going out with a friend tonight."

He lingered awkwardly for a moment, then sat down on the edge of the bed and further inquired, "Where are you guys headed to?" as he watched her apply a sultry smoke to her eyelids that he hadn't seen in years.

"Oh, ummm – my friend has a friend who's opening an art exhibit tonight, so he invited me to come along with him. Fancy suit-and-tie stuff – you wouldn't really like it anyways…"

Andrew nodded quietly and watched his wife continue to transform before his very eyes until she finally turned to him and asked, "Hey, while you're here – can you help me with something?"

"Sure, no problem," he perked up with a smile. "What do you need?"

"There's a gift bag in the closet. Can you grab it for me? I'm running late and he's going to be here any minute, so I don't want to keep him waiting…"

Stepping into their walk-in closet, Andrew took a moment to scan the shelves until he finally noticed a glossy bag with white and black letters leaning up against the wall by his feet. Carrying it back out to the bed, he removed a fancy box with the same letters – appearing to be a French word that he couldn't pronounce – on the lid.

"Thank-you!" his wife replied curtly as she took the box from his hands and opened it out on the bed to reveal a strikingly seductive set of black lingerie, which instantly reminded Andrew where he had seen the French word before because it was the name of a very high-end boutique in the mall that the couple never visited because they couldn't afford to shop there.

"Where'd you get those???" he asked curiously as he watched his wife marvel over the silky smooth garments within as she anxiously sorted through the carefully wrapped box.

"Oh, they were a gift…" Kate sang nonchalantly as she laid each item out on their bed with the utmost of care, first pairing the luxurious silk stockings together, then the garter belt, and finally the matching bra and panties that immediately caught Andrew's attention as they almost seemed to have a shimmer of leather in them.

Andrew took a deep breath as he bit his lip looking down at the sexy lingerie, then asked as he felt his heart rate increase, "…are they from that doctor friend of yours?"

Kate smiled warmly as she looked up at him.

"Yes, Marcus … err, *Dr. Powers* bought them for me…" she explained with a smile as she bit her lip, then dropped her towel to the floor and picked up the garter belt to situate it around her hips.

"If you'd like to watch me put them on, you can sit there in my chair at the vanity…" she suggested, again without looking up, as she focused on closing the tiny hasp of the belt behind her back, taking note herself of the sexy patches of smooth, black leather that were built into the lacy garment.

Andrew's eyes randomly dropped to the floor as he heard his wife's comments, and then without further reaction, he simply stood up from the corner of the bed and walked over to the vanity where the glosses and shades that she had been putting on her lips and face were still laid out from moments ago. He looked away to clear a small lump that had been growing in his throat, then turned the chair back in the direction of his wife to watch her get dressed…

Kate paid her husband no mind as she meticulously straightened the garters down her front and backside, then reached for the first of the two silk stockings to run up her short, but shapely legs. The smooth silk leggings felt like nothing she'd worn before as she guided the exotic material up her freshly shaven legs until they came to rest mid-thigh.

It wasn't until she had donned both stockings and was proceeding to affix each of the six garters from around her belt that Andrew's eyes were drawn in to notice that she had also shaven *between her legs* as well, but he said not a word as he continued to watch her work…

Next picking up the new bra from its place on their bed, she took another moment to admire its smooth, black shine up close before slipping into the straps and lifting her breasts into it to reveal that it was actually only a half-bra that barely covered her nipples and left exposed the top majority of her gorgeous breasts as the smooth, leather-like material cupped them from below.

Stepping over to her husband backwards, she glanced back and asked him, "Do you mind?" as she gestured to the bra clasp at the small of her back.

Andrew reached up with both hands and quickly clipped the clasps together, curious to the touch of the garment's material for only a split second before Kate stepped away again as she adjusted the straps over her shoulders.

Finally looking down at the dainty pair of jet black panties – the only item left from the designer box – Kate turned her attention to the full-length mirror with her backside to her husband as she stepped into the seductive underwear and slid them up her legs, smiling ever so slightly as she pulled them taut against her pussy that had she had shaved bare especially for him, the ties of the panties coming to rest up over her garters as she giggled and thought to herself, *"Easy access for later…"*

Taking a step back as she relished her irresistible figure in her new lingerie, Kate called out to her husband once again, "Hey, there's a black garment bag in the closet, too – can you do me a favor and grab that as well?"

Kate closed her eyes for just a moment as her husband disappeared again into the closet, imagining Marcus' firm hands pulling her body into his until Andrew re-emerged with the bag in hand, which she directed him to open so that she could finish getting dressed.

The smell of leather hit him like a drug the moment Andrew zipped open the bag, and a moment later as he pulled the garment bag off the hanger to reveal its contents, it became abundantly clear why. Inside was a decadent black leather dress, tight and form fitting that looked like it would barely cover her garters. He felt his breathing quicken as he looked over the dress and then glanced back to his lingerie-clad wife, who was quick to prod him along by cattily saying, "Come on – are you going to help or not?! Take it off the hanger so that I can put it on…"

Taking the buttery soft leather of the shoulder straps in his hands, Andrew carefully undid the small zipper that ran down the back of the dress, then once it was fully opened, removed the wooden hanger that it had come on and threw the hanger onto the bed. He lingered over it a bit longer as his wife walked over while he held it out, then stepped into it and graciously slid the dress upwards until she could get her arms under the shoulder straps.

"So … was *this* a gift, too?" he barely croaked out as he watched the exquisite leather take form around his wife's figure.

"…I guess so…" she only half-answered him as she admired the transformation taking place in the mirror and trying to hold back just how wonderful the cool leather felt against her skin, knowing that her husband likely had the hard-on of a lifetime standing nearby.

"Zip me up," she commented as she turned her back to him, gesturing again for him to help where she wasn't able to reach as the fitted leather slid into place underneath her arms and seemed to sync perfectly with her bra to show off a copious amount of her cleavage.

Just as the zipper reached its home, she continued without missing a beat, "Now go in the closet and get my shoes – I want the tall, strappy ones with the platforms … the black leather ones."

Andrew disappeared and fumbled around in the closet for a few minutes while Kate smoothed out the leather down her body, amused as she came to the bumps that were each of her six garters, both because the dress actually managed to cover them in the first place, but also because they could still just barely be made out through the tight leather in a surprisingly sexy sort of way.

When her husband finally emerged, the shoes of her picking dangling from one hand, she heard him make a comment under his breath as he reached to hand them to her…

"What – he didn't just **buy you new shoes,** *too?!"*

Kate turned and gave him a snide look, then told him, "You can leave the shoes on the bed – I don't need your help anymore."

Andrew gave a flabbergasted look and attempted to protest, "But I … I …"

…though Kate was quick to cut him off and raised her voice, *"Put my shoes on the bed and wait for me downstairs!"*

Shocked at the tone in his wife's voice, Andrew carefully set her shoes on the bed next to the empty lingerie box, then quickly walked out of the bedroom, closing the door behind him…

Letting out a big sigh and rolling her eyes, Kate turned her attention back to the mirror and smiled again as she saw her marvelous figure in the form-fitting leather, taking a couple of turns to enjoy the view from behind as well before remembering the shoes that her husband had left for her on the bed. Slipping into the tall platforms and buckling the numerous straps around her ankles, she melted as she saw what the extra five inches did to elongate her legs and bring even more attention to all of the right areas.

When her fantasies began to drift again to Marcus' hands groping her through the tight leather throughout the night, frantic for any place that the two could duck away inside the gallery for a little *naughty-naughty*, Kate had to snap herself back into reality by reminding herself that *the real thing* was only moments away and would be knocking at her door any moment!

Putting a few final touches on her makeup and then throwing some essentials in the black leather handbag with silver accents, she knew that she didn't dare tell her husband that *Marcus had actually bought the matching purse for her, too* as she slung the bag's silver chain over her shoulder and took one final look in the mirror.

Ever since she had casually mentioned to Marcus that her husband had a fetish for leather, he had been dropping comments about how amazing she would look in it, though she had declined every last one … **until now.**

Ready to move past the evening's minor hiccup and into *more enjoyable* parts of her night, Kate took one last opportunity to spritz herself with a lovely, feminine bouquet in each of the areas that her man was sure to notice, then slowly walked down the spiral stairs to the main floor where she found Andrew waiting patiently for her on the edge of his seat in their living room. After walking to the window and glancing outside to ensure that her date hadn't already arrived, Kate gingerly walked back to where her husband was sitting to vent her frustrations from earlier's incident…

"That was a very rude comment that you made earlier," Kate scolded him as she towered over him in her five-inch heels. "Marcus is a very generous man, and you should be grateful that he buys me these nice things that you're not able to afford yourself."

Andrew looked out at the leather-clad figure before him, hardly believing that it was his own wife, his eyes first dropping down to the strappy, black platform heels on her feet that he'd been asked to retrieve for her and then tracing his was up her delicate, silky legs until they disappeared underneath the edge of the tight, leather dress that followed her figure all the way up to a magnificent display of her breasts that left very little to the imagination.

"I know - I'm sorry…" he croaked out as he reached her

eyes that were piercing back at him, her smug smile in deep red seemingly the only acceptance that he would be receiving back.

After he hung his head again, his eyes drifting back to the leather heels that admittedly he had encouraged her to buy to satisfy a shoe fetish of his own, Kate smirked at her husband's act of submission, then asked him sarcastically, "Would you like a better opportunity to apologize???"

He looked up at her towering over him from his seat again, then nodded his head yes, to which she amusingly replied with a chuckle in her voice, "Get down on the floor and kiss my shoes…"

Looking back at her with a raised eyebrow, they both turned their heads a moment later to see a pair of headlights turn into their driveway.

"That's him," Kate prodded. "You'd better do it now if you're going to…"

Glancing back at her one last time, enough that the image of his wife looking down her nose at him would be burned into his memory for days, Andrew sheepishly let out a long sigh, then got down on his hands and knees on the carpet until his wife's delicate toes were squarely in front of him. Taking notice of the sweet smell of his favorite perfume of hers blending with the undeniable leather that encapsulated her, he inched his lips down close to the silk stocking that wrapped her feet underneath the tantalizing straps of her shoes.

"I said kiss **my shoes,** *not* **my feet…"** she warned, snickering to herself as she thought that maybe Marcus had been right about all of the things that he had said about her husband after all. She grinned as she watched him carefully caressing the sexy, leather straps that held the platform shoe to her foot, then laughed again to herself as she saw him ready to move to the other foot and sharply interrupted, *"No, why don't you kiss* **the bottom** *of this one…"* before lifting her right leg up above Andrew's head, impressed as he did exactly as he was told and brought his lips to the opposite side of the platform from where her toes rested, gently pressing down until the back of his head was held firmly to the floor by her foot.

Just then the doorbell rang, and with that Kate jerked her foot away and announced, "Time to go!" as she gingerly walked away from her husband laying on the floor, thinking to herself, *"…right where you belong…"* as she knew his eyes followed her every last step to the door.

With one hand on the handle, she turned back and told him, "I almost forgot to tell you – Veronica is going to be stopping by later to drop off something for me. Do me a favor and don't give her any trouble…"

Before he could ask or say another word, Kate had opened the door and added, *"I'll probably be home late – don't wait up!"* before closing the door behind her and nearly falling into the arms of her date, Marcus, on the front porch.

"You look *incredible – I told you* that you could pull this off without a hitch!" he told her as he wrapped his arms around her, with Kate quick to run a hand up his washboard abs inside of his designer suit while she savored in the newfound knowledge that no matter how sweet leather felt on a woman's body, it felt even better between her and the touch of a strong man.

The two intertwined flirtatiously on the front porch, only a couple of dozen feet away from where Kate's husband still lay confused on the living room floor, with Marcus already playing with her garters like it was going to be a fun night, until finally they broke away and she raced him back to his car, teasing, *"Come on, let's get going — I have something* **very interesting** *that I want to tell you!"*

* * * * * * * * * *

A couple of hours passed before Andrew heard the doorbell ring again that evening. Unsure of just how his evening could possibly get any stranger, he opened the door to find his wife's nursing co-worker, Veronica, just as Kate had told him to expect on her way out the door…

Welcoming her inside, he didn't think much of the plastic lock box that she was carrying, still in her scrubs after just having finished another 12-hour shift, though enough to bring a smile to his face all the same. The young girl chatted casually with him for a few minutes after setting the box down on the kitchen counter, batting her eyes and pretending to care about whatever he had to say as she'd found long ago worked quite well for her whenever she needed to get something from a member of the opposite sex.

"So are you ready to get this over with?" she asked him with a giggle as she drummed her fingers anxiously on the top of the closed box.

"Oh, is that what you're dropping off for Kate?" he asked unknowingly as he leaned up against the opposite counter. "I don't really know what it is, but apparently it's important so I guess you can just leave it there or wherever…"

Veronica giggled as she glanced up at him, then down at the box, commenting, "Well, it *is* pretty important, but it's *not exactly* something that I can just leave here!"

"Ok, well, I won't *mess with it or anything,* if that's what you're concerned about…" Andrew grumbled, flashing back to his *incident* earlier with his wife and thinking that maybe she had somehow spoken to Veronica since then.

"That's *not* what I'm worried about…" Veronica laughed as she flipped open the clasps on the lid of the box, adding, "…in fact, *that's kind of the whole point of this in the first place!*"

The blonde continued chuckling to herself as she began to unload the box onto the counter, with Andrew looking on to see her unpacking a series of what appeared to be long, silver bands of varying length that somehow fit together, followed by a strange, tube-like device and a couple of other odd-shaped pieces, and then finally a shiny, silver padlock that was currently unlocked. Once all of the pieces had been emptied from the padded box, Veronica set it off to the side and began lining some of the pieces up and clicking them together until finally Andrew chimed in and asked, "So what is all this stuff???"

"This," Veronica announced proudly as she held up parts of the device that were slowly starting to resemble what Kate had picked out in the pictures, *"is your new* **chastity belt!"**

She giggled and batted her eyes at him as she continued with her work while he stood there baffled for a moment from the other side of the kitchen counter, then replied back, "Wait, *my what???"*

The girl then put down the belt and smiled at him more directly.

"Your *chastity belt* – your wife ordered it for you…"

"I don't understand," he told her. "I've never heard of any of this before, and why are *you here* to give it to me now if it's supposed to be from *my wife???"* Andrew did his best not to raise his voice in confusion after what happened earlier, but he'd never heard of such a thing before and it just didn't make any sense…

"No problem!" Veronica quipped back with a cute grin. "We can do a quick Q&A first if that's what it's going to take. Second question first – I'm here because your wife is *otherwise occupied* tonight … *so* **that one's** *easy enough.* As for *what it is,* well, let's just say that it's designed to *help* guys like you … it's a little personal, I know, but *down there…"*

"Huh?!" Andrew retorted back at the girl. "I don't have any problems *down there!!!"* he emphasized, glancing down at his own crotch before looking back at the blue-eyed girl in a thoroughly bewildered state.

Veronica just smiled and pressed forward.

"That's really none of my business," she told him sweetly. "I'm really just here to help you try it on, and then maybe you can ask some more of these questions *to your wife* when she gets home *tomorrow…"*

The girl then leaned in closer to him and told him, *"Look, I know that this is a little* **weird,** *but it'll all be over a lot quicker if* *you just* **play along** *and then I can get out of here…"*

With that Veronica winked at the man and gave him another smile as she knelt down in front of him and reached for his zipper, and then without a word of protest pulled both his pants and boxers down in one fell swoop to reveal a slowly growing erection underneath. The girl tapped on his curiously-aroused member with her finger as she saw it getting larger before her very eyes, then appeared to measure it between her finger and thumb before giving it a shrug and standing up to face the dropped-jaw man once again.

"It's ok," she pretended to blush as she looked down at his erection and then back up at him again, *"I'm kind of* **used to** *this sort of thing by now!"* Walking back over to the counter while Andrew just stared at her speechless with his pants around his ankles, she quickly returned with one of the larger, silver tubes, knelt down and held it up to his erect penis before commenting, "This should work, *but we're going to have to do something about* **your arousal** *first…"*

Andrew turned a deep shade of red as Veronica just giggled while she looked at him, then took a few steps over and started sorting through the freezer compartment of their refrigerator.

"Now this is going to be *a little cold…*" she laughed as she revealed that in her hand she held a couple of pieces of ice only moments before touching them directly to his erect shaft and then slowly running them down the sides before eventually holding the frozen pieces against the underside of his balls.

"Just take a few deep breaths and relax for me," she sang as if he were one of her patients. *"It will all be over soon…"*

Andrew was too embarrassed to look down and too confused by the whole situation to think as he felt the chilling sensations around his shaft and balls and even every so often along the tip of his penis as well until he could only imagine that they'd all but shriveled up into nothing! Still Veronica held the ice firmly in place until it had completely melted, when she finally announced as if it were a major achievement, *"Woohoo - now we can get back to work!"*

"I still don't … understand…" he attempted to sheepishly stammer out as she stood up momentarily to walk back to the counter, but Veronica just tuned him out and returned with the same silver tube as before, this time taking him even further off guard as without a word of explanation she took the tube in one hand and slipped it over his now-cold and shriveled, formerly erect penis with her free hand, and then slid the tube all the way up until it touched his body…

Next, taking the full tube in one hand, she looked up and giggled as she said, "Oops! I just realized that this would be a lot easier if you were *over here…*" pulling him by his enclosed dick with his pants and underwear still around his ankles until they were closer to the counter with the rest of the parts on it.

Then laughing, *"Stay!"* to herself as she let go of the tube momentarily and reached up for the rest of the steel straps that would make up the belt itself, Veronica made little work of looping the outside ring around Andrew's waist and clicking it temporarily into place before he inevitably tried to ask questions again while she worked to fit the front shield in-line with the strap that was intended to come between his legs…

"Wait – now hold on," he protested, though Veronica quickly shut him up with a surprisingly effective,

"Sssshhhh!" adding a second later, "Trust me, you don't want me to *pinch anything* down here, so just *hold on* and I'll be with you in a minute!"

It was all that he could to do just shake his head and stand there in his own kitchen bowlegged as the blonde was on her knees doing what he had no idea at that point. A few more minutes passed while he felt what he thought was the straps slowly getting tighter around his waist, then between his legs, with the metal cup that she had been messing with now cradling his balls while his penis strangely pointed downwards inside of the tube that little did he know was about to become its new long-term home.

Looking off into the other room, his mind wandering as he felt boggled with whatever Kate had come up with for him this time, he wasn't paying attention when Veronica reached up and nabbed the silver padlock that had been sitting open on the counter, nor at that point did he make any connection of that unique clicking sound between his legs among all of the others that the girl had been making…

"Now just a couple of last things…" Veronica muttered under her breath as she got up and looked around the box until she found what appeared to be a small hex wrench, then grabbed her phone and knelt back in front of her confused host once more. After flipping through her phone for a moment, she appeared to read something that made her chuckle. Then glancing back up at Andrew and shrugging to herself with a nod of her head, the girl set her phone down on the floor, located the hidden slot in the bottom of the belt that she'd been told to look for, and inserted the tiny wrench and began to turn it against the already snug belt.

"This might sting a little…" she warned just as she heard his first gasp and felt him wince before her. She counted in her head, *"One … two … and then* **one from me…"** as she twisted the tiny wrench before finally removing it and looking up to see the grimace on Andrew's face and the damage that she had caused.

"What was that?!" he exclaimed as he felt a bit of water in his eyes, shifting back and forth in an attempt to get the sharp pain between his legs to dissipate.

Without looking up at him, Veronica then took her phone in hand once again and abruptly asked him, *"Can you hold still for like. two. seconds?!"* as she leaned back with the phone to his crotch, then clicked the button on the side to take a photo of her final work.

Then standing up and looking him over with the first judgmental smirk that he'd seen from her all night, Veronica commented, "If you can relax a little bit, some of the discomfort might start to go away…" as she took the extra pieces off the counter along with the tiny wrench in her hand and placed them all back inside the padded box, closing the heavy-duty hinges once again, this time double-checking them to make sure that they wouldn't open again on their own.

After verifying that the contents of the box would be secure, the blonde stepped around to the side of the counter opposite Andrew and with her back towards the door before she spoke again…

"So, yeah…" she visibly laughed at him for the first time since she'd been seemingly giggling *with him* earlier, "…you should be able to fit that thing underneath your clothes, but it sounds like you might want to take your pants off and *just get used to it for a while* before adding in any additional pressure…"

"What is this thing???" he asked her yet again as she looked

down at his groin and did his best to not move his hips, which seemed to make the pain that specifically seemed to run along his dick and balls much worse.

"I told you – *it's a chastity belt* … haven't you ever heard of one, even in the movies???"

Andrew shook his head no as he confusingly stared back at the girl.

"They're for keeping people from *having sex,*" she explained with a small hint of sympathy, "or in your case, *to keep you from* **masturbating** *while your wife is out on the town…*"

Reading the baffled, yet harmless look on his face, Veronica cautiously came back around the counter and pointed out with her finger, "You saw that tube that I was playing with? Your cock is in *that,* and then your balls are actually *down here below* at the bottom of this steel pouch."

She tapped on the bottom of the cage with her finger, then immediately realized what she had done and looked up with an apologetic, *"Sorry!"* before explaining, "Now you'll still be able to pee *through here,* but you'll need to be *sitting down* to do it. Poop comes out *the same place it did before* – you just have to *check the band afterwards* to make sure you clean off whatever gets stuck to the hole…"

"Oh yeah," she added as she stood up and looked him in the eye, "and those sharp pains that you're feeling??? That's a *feature* that your wife had to ask for specially. I don't know if you noticed, but some of those other parts in the box had *smooth insides* to them – the ones that I didn't use. *Instead,* the ones that I used have these *tiny, needle-sized spikes* that run along the insides … that little wrench is what I used to engage them, and you can engage them on *up to 5 levels* for varying … well, you know."

"I got a text from Kate saying that you had *misbehaved* earlier, and to engage them two turns. And then she said that if you were *sassy or resistant with me* at any time, I was to turn them up a third…"

Andrew winced as he turned his head up to look at the ceiling as he closed his eyes in pain, then told her back quietly, *"I didn't mean to be disrespectful – I just didn't know what you were doing…"*

Raising an eyebrow despite his obvious pain, Veronica shot right back, "You mean to tell me that *if I told you first* what I was going to do, *that you would've just gone along with it?!"*

For the second time that evening, Andrew uttered the words, "I'm sorry…" to a woman, though it was debatable which one he had meant more – the apology to his wife or the one just then to the woman whom he was still hoping would offer him a hint of mercy.

"I'll tell you what…" Veronica said with a sympathetic tone that piqued Andrew's hope by just a hair. "I can't really do anything about *your wife's turns,* but what if I give you an opportunity to *earn back* the turn that I added for myself???"

The man shrugged his shoulders as he looked back at the attractive blonde and told her, "Sure – that would be great … anything would be better than nothing! What do you want me to do – *kiss your shoes?"*

Veronica held her hand up to cover her mouth as she began laughing at his suggestion, quickly throwing back, *"No! Is* **that** *what she made you do?! That must've been a sight to see…"*

The girl giggled while he hung his head in shame, although thankfully the setting did seem to make the sharp pains around his cock and balls go down significantly. Andrew stood there in silence as Veronica thought for a moment, then looked back at him with a gleam in her eye as she said, "You know what? I kind of *do* like that whole *kissing thing,* but I've got something *a little better in mind!"*

"Have you ever **kissed somebody's ass?"**

"Oh, this will be fun!" she announced as she took him by the hand and led him over to the carpeted floor of the living room nearby, *pants and underwear still around his ankles,* and instructed him, "Now get down on your knees behind me…"

As far as Andrew could see, he was certainly in no place to argue at that point, so he carefully knelt down on the carpet not far from where he had been kissing the bottom of his wife's shoe earlier.

Once he was in place, Veronica turned back and playfully whispered in his ear, "I don't recommend *getting aroused* by this or you're probably going to be in a lot of pain afterwards!"

Turning back around as she giggled to herself, the young

blonde then loosened the drawstring on her scrub pants and a moment later they fell to the floor around her ankles, leaving her ass maybe six inches from his face and the only thing separating the two a skimpy, pink thong that already made him take a deep breath.

After she then reached down and innocently pulled her panties down to her ankles so that her perfectly round ass was staring him right in the face, she explained his next steps, "Now this is a *hands free* exercise, so inch forward until you're *right in my ass* and then take your hands and hold onto my ankles…"

"It's probably good that you get some practice in — something tells me that you're going to be doing **a lot of this** *in the future!"*

Andrew took another pair of deep breaths to try and center himself, but he already found himself growing aroused simply at the sound of Veronica's voice, much less the bare ass hanging in front of him, and so in an attempt to simply push through and get it over with, he shimmied forward just enough to put the girl's ankles within grasp and then also brought his lips to her white butt cheeks all at once. The girl stood there motionless for a moment, then after feeling her arching her back and pushing her ass against his lips he assumed that he had done it correctly until she spoke up again.

"So here's the thing," she reported as she flexibly stretched back and forth in front of him, "that's good for *a first effort,* but if you *really* want to show someone that you *respect them…*"

"*…and trust me,* **your wife** *will* **love** *this…*"

"*…you kiss their asshole.*"

Waiting for a couple of moments, she soon prodded, "Well come on – *do it!*" and the next second, she happily felt the man's lips resting squarely against her asshole, kissing as a gentleman would kiss until she added, "It's ok to give it a little *tongue…*" and her grin grew bigger still as she felt the man further humiliating himself behind her without even realizing it.

Veronica let Andrew continue tasting her ass for a solid 30 seconds, amused as he obediently clung to her ankles tightly while his tongue humbly explored the tight folds of the girl's asshole before she finally reached down with one fell swoop and pulled her underwear and pants back up while also knocking *her anal suitor* back onto the floor.

"I never said anything about **them** *respecting* **you** *back…"* she chuckled to herself as she grabbed her phone from the counter and turned to walk towards the front door, adding under her breath, *"You really are kind of a pushover – no wonder he had such an easy time winning her over…"* as she walked away.

"Wait a minute!" Andrew shouted after her, lying awkwardly on the floor with his pants binding his ankles together and in too much pain between his legs to pursue her regardless. "I thought we had a deal!"

Veronica laughed as she shouted back, "I don't even have the wrench anymore – it's locked inside that box, so you'll have to take it up with her when she gets home!"

"But you lied to me…" he whined as he watched the beautiful, young girl stepping through her front door.

Surprisingly, the girl turned back and offered one final piece of sage-like wisdom before she shut the door, *"Sorry – sometimes a girl just likes to get her ass kissed…"*

Veronica laughed to herself and spoke out loud, "Wow – *that* was interesting!" as she casually walked back to her car and got in, knowing all too well that he had no intention of coming after her … not that there was anything that she could do for him at that point, anyways…

Just before pulling out of the couple's driveway, Veronica sent two text messages to her friend, Marcus – the first one included her photo of the chastity belt securely in place, with the caption, *"Mission Accomplished!"*

The second simply added, *"P.S. Tell Kate that her husband's kind of a kiss-ass, in a fun way..."*

* * * * * * * * *

Kate's pussy throbbed as Marcus' eight inch cock slammed into her from behind while she knelt in the center of his bed, her new dress now relegated to hanging over the chair in the corner, though she still wore the lingerie that he had bought her especially for that night. Their collective grunts and her cries of passion echoed through the room as they both finally climaxed simultaneously, with Marcus' warm cum filling her insides as she dug her nails recklessly into the sheets and leaned back into his girth all the more.

 "Oh my god!" Kate moaned as she crumpled into a pile

on the bed and was moments later scooped up into the man's strong arms as he slid onto the sheets beside her. "I can't tell you the last time I was fucked like that…"

Marcus chuckled as he was catching his breath, "Maybe *the last time* that we were together???"

"You know what I mean…" she jabbed at him playfully as she slid one of her stocking-clad legs between his and nibbled gently at his lips as the tremors in her body disappeared into the horizon. As her free hand slowly came to rest on the man's firm stomach, Kate took a moment to stare into his deep, blue eyes before nestling herself into the crook of his arm, looking up at him dreamily, and giggling…

"I **really** *enjoy fucking you!"*

The doctor grinned proudly and touched his thumb to her cheek as he replied, *"I really like fucking* **you,** *too!"*

"I'm just glad that you were open to it…"

Kate confessed as she snuggled closer to her lover, "You know, I was a little surprised about the whole thing, but it's ended up being an *amazing* amount of fun! I never would've thought that *cuckolding* would be such a turn-on for a married woman…"

"Believe it or not," he looked back at her, "it's actually been a huge turn-on for *me, too.*"

Marcus ran his fingers tenderly over the woman's belly, tracing a line along the top of the smooth, leather-like garter belt that he had bought especially for her.

"Really?" she responded with a tone of genuine surprise in her voice as she enjoyed the gentle touches on her mid-section. "This isn't just about scoring with that hot nurse who always flirts with you at work?!" she asked with a laugh.

Marcus grinned himself as he shook his head.

"That doesn't *hurt,*" he laughed, "but why do you think that I bought you *all of this, and that dress???*" He ran his hand down along the straps of her garters, coming to rest on the silky stockings that she had worn just for him.

Kate beamed as she turned her head into his side to hide her smile, "I can't *tell you* how hot it was today for me to get all dressed up for you! It felt so naughty – making my husband *watch me* as I slipped into this sexy lingerie that *another man* had bought for me. I couldn't believe that he actually stood for it all … it kind of made me want to *push him* even farther…"

Marcus felt his manhood stir once again as he noted the fiendish look in the woman's eyes.

"So, how do you think our other little *experiment* went tonight???" he asked, eluding to the chastity belt that he had encouraged Kate to order for her husband.

"I don't know!" she thought with a grin. "I still have a hard time picturing him *letting someone else* do that to him, although I did kind of have him wrapped around my little finger when I left with you earlier this evening…"

At that point Marcus reached over to the nightstand and snagged up his phone, after which he promptly noticed the two new messages that Veronica had sent him. "No shit…" he exclaimed as he pulled up the photo, then handed the phone over to Kate so that she could get a better look for herself.

"Well isn't *that* interesting!" she laughed as she looked at the photo that Veronica had taken just after locking Andrew into the new chastity device. She let out a loud sigh as she admired the photo, zooming in for a preview of what it looked like up close before finally holding his phone up again so that Marcus could see the image, too, as she asked him, *"How bad do you think the spikes hurt???"*

The man thought for a moment, then told her earnestly, "Probably quite a bit. They're supposed to be like 26-gauge needles – *dozens of them* – not long enough to break the skin, but if he becomes aroused with them, they *are* all along his balls and shaft…"

"…and even in *the head* in that attachment that you got, I think…" he added with a slight shudder.

"Either way, you *did* say that *he deserves it,* didn't you?" he asked the adulterous woman curiously.

"Yeah, I guess that I did," Kate admitted as she pondered the image of dozens of tiny needles impaling her husband's penis, more *curious* than anything else as she considered the amount of pain that they could be capable of inflicting.

"You're going to start seeing a changed man out of him

now, I tell you," Marcus said as the two continued to look at the chastity photo, then laughed together when he flipped over to the second message that Veronica had sent about Andrew *kissing her ass.*

"I already have," she told him with a smug look on her face, adding, *"He knows that I'm fooling around with you…"* as the slightest smile crossed her face.

"…and yet tonight you had him **kissing your high heels** *because he was* **inadvertently rude to me!"** Marcus posed to the wedded woman in his arms with a haughty laugh.

"Hey, I can't let him **disrespect my boyfriend** *like that!"* she threw back with a giggle as the two nonchalantly took pleasure in Kate's newfound air of dominance.

As they continued to bask in the wake of their throes of passion, reveling in the thought of what was building between the two of them, and even her husband, too, though arguably against his will, Kate began to muse as she ran her own fingers across the expensive lingerie that had become a devout symbol of their scandalous game…

"It all felt so *electrifying* today – slipping into these smooth stockings and this seductive garter belt while he sat only a few feet away. I could tell that he was uncomfortable, but he didn't protest a word as I so openly paraded my new lingerie in front of him that could've only meant one thing. And then when I had him bring out *the dress* – I thought he was just going to *melt* as his hands nervously held it out so that I could climb into it … *for someone else.* I knew that he would've loved nothing more than to touch me and kiss me in that beautiful leather, *and in a way I felt a little bit sorry for him…"*

"…but then he back talked you…" Marcus led her with a small smile.

"…but then he back talked me, and in that very moment I just felt this rush that made me want to make him *suffer."*

"I kind of wish that he had been wearing his chastity belt *then,"* Kate continued, "because I would've loved to see the all-encompassing effect that it would've had on him – his wife towering before him in leather and high heels that he would just die to touch, making herself beautiful so that she can go out and be romanced and fucked by a real man, all the while he's kneeling on the ground begging to even kiss the shoes that he once bought her, his pathetic dick locked up in chastity because he's unable to please her any longer…"

"And I'd remind him just how *small and insignificant* it is compared to *my lover's cock…*"

"And then I'd look down at him and *laugh* as he licks the very bottoms of my shoes because that's the only place where he's worthy to kiss me anymore!"

"Oh my god?!" she exclaimed as she found herself climbing back over her lover and easily slipping his well-aroused cock between her folds. *"Why am I getting* **so wet** *thinking about* **humiliating my husband** *like this?!"*

Marcus grinned as he slipped inside of the woman once again, telling her, *"It becomes you, dear — there's no sense in denying it…"*

"By the way," he added as she began to roll her hips against him as he toyed with her nipples gingerly, "there are all sorts of *other* humiliating things that we can do to your husband that will make what we've done so far look like kids stuff…"

Kate groaned, *"I'm all ears!"* as she tipped her head back

while she began to slam herself down on his cock harder and harder with each thrust, savoring each drop of pleasure and pain that seeped through her nipples in his hands while visions of her husband, at home and alone on his knees in his chastity belt, drifted to the back of her mind to make way for more urgent pleasures.

* * * * * * * * *

Meanwhile back at her home, Andrew sat alone at his wife's computer, reading through the dozens of e-mails and pictures that she had exchanged with her lover over the past several months, unable to look away, and unable to deny the throbbing pain underneath the belt as he feigned arousal against the torturous spikes with each new image of them together that cemented itself inside of his mind…

Her New Cuckold
...Teased

Her New Cuckold ...
Teased

"Something's going to have to change – we can't live *like this!*"

"Well, why not?" Kate responded to her husband with a demure smile as she leisurely took another bite of her sandwich while he paced back and forth frustratingly in their kitchen.

"Why not?!" Andrew protested to his wife defiantly. "You locked *a chastity belt* around my cock, Kate!!!"

"Ok, two things…" she pointed out as she dabbed a napkin to her lips. "Number One - *I* didn't lock it on you, *Veronica did.* And Number Two – *don't use the word* **cock** *to describe yourself because you* **clearly** *don't know the difference between* **a real one** *and* **that thing** *you have…*"

Andrew stopped dead in his tracks and looked back at her shocked, but couldn't find the words to respond next.

"Besides, it doesn't have to be *all bad!*" she countered before he had a chance to recover from her quite vivid bitch slap. "This whole thing could actually be *kind of fun* – if you'll just learn to accept it…"

He continued to stare back at her hurt and confused as he shook his head and asked, "How in the world am I supposed to *enjoy* my wife sleeping with another man?!"

Kate just chuckled as she finished the last bite on her plate and pushed it away from her before standing up and walking over to the fridge. As she retrieved the pitcher of iced tea and refilled her glass on the island between them, she offered nonchalantly, "I don't know yet, but I'm sure we can figure out something!"

After she slid the pitcher back into its place in the refrigerator, Kate walked over to her husband and without warning, gave him a series of pats on his groin that she knew would drive the spikes that had yet to be retracted from the previous weekend painfully into his limp dick. As he winced under her hand without saying a word, she leaned in closer to him and whispered, "Don't think that I didn't notice that hard-on of yours when you were down on your hands and knees, kissing my shoes before I went out with my lover Saturday night … this new role may end up suiting you more than you're ready to admit."

As she walked away, she called over her shoulder, "Now be a dear and take care of my dishes for me – I think I'm going to enjoy some time out in the sun…"

Hanging his head as the newfound pain made his short walk to the table where she had ate quite the chore, Andrew obediently took his wife's plate and fork over to the sink where he began to rise them off before depositing them into the dishwasher when he looked up to hear her add on while standing in the doorway leading out to the patio…

"You know, you're right, honey – something *is* going to have to change around here."

"And the thing is, *I'm not going to be subtle about it anymore…*"

Andrew spent the next several hours in heavy contemplation as his adulterous wife lounged about just outside on their patio. After having rinsed the few random dishes lying around and turning on the dishwasher, he thought long and hard about this unconscionable scenario that she had forced upon him, and a million questions flooded his head that earlier he had been too overwhelmed with anger and confusion to even consider…

Why was she doing this to him?

What had driven her to find passion in the arms of another?

Was it something that **he had done** *to drive her away?*

What if **he wasn't capable** *of making his own wife happy anymore???*

He tried to put his nervous frustrations to good use while Kate enjoyed her alone time by tidying up the rest of the kitchen, then proceeding on to the living and family rooms until he had made an impact in nearly every room in the house, addressing everything from the messy bed to the laundry to even cleaning up his wife's vanity where she had humiliated him by dressing up for another man in front of him only a few days prior.

Wandering into the couple's closet, his eyes immediately fell to the decadent, short leather dress that she had worn out on that same fateful night, initially reaching out to feel the cool leather beneath his fingertips that had seemingly felt just out of his reach when he was helping her get dressed earlier, yet instinctively he jerked his hand back as if she were watching from just over his shoulder, scolding him, *"No – that's not* **for you…"** as his eyes dropped to the floor and his gaze was instead directed to her shiny, platform heels that had been left nearby instead…

After doing all that he could around the house shy of firing up the vacuum cleaner and risk disturbing his lounging wife, Andrew decided to make more of an effort to get back in his love's good graces, and after doing a quick bit of research online, he carefully and methodically gathered up the leather dress back into its original garment bag along with the special lingerie that she had worn as well with the intent of dropping them all off at the local dry cleaners while he made a trip to the local market in search of some fresh meats and vegetables for dinner. Finding that with a little extra, they could expedite their work so that he could have the leatherwear back in her closet that same night, he proudly took to task planning a special menu that he knew his wife would love to help keep his mind off of all of the other immoral thoughts that had been bombarding his head.

When Kate finally came back into the house as the sun was setting, she couldn't help but notice all of the work that her husband had accomplished that afternoon as she found him busily chopping away in the kitchen with a myriad of wonderfully smells wafting forth...

"Mmmmm – what's for dinner?" she asked with a smile as she approached to further examine her husband's handiwork.

"Spiced tilapia with fresh corn and peppers, paired with a crisp White Bordeaux," he announced without looking up as he focused on dicing the peppers in front of him.

"Well it smells *wonderful!*" she commented, then asking, "About how long until everything is ready?"

"Maybe half an hour at best?" Andrew replied, finally looking up to catch his wife's approving gaze.

"Ok – I think I might draw a quick bath…" she told him as she turned away and made her way up the stairs to their bedroom without looking back, though unable to shake off the smug grin that grew on her face once she had disappeared from his field of vision. Her sentiment was only bolstered as she walked in to find their bed made and the bedroom generally tidied up as well, but it wasn't until she stepped into the walk-in closet and flipped on the light to find the garment bag now returned around her breathtaking gift dress *with the dry cleaner's tag dated that day hanging from the zipper* that she stopped and said aloud to herself in amusement, *"Well isn't* **that** *interesting…"*

Taking then to the bathroom and turning the water on high, Kate tossed one of her strawberry-scented bath bombs into the rapidly rising water and a few minutes later sunk in herself up to her neck, the hot water unleashing a tirade of emotions as she found herself pondering a world where her husband actually *accepted* this newfound desire that she had uncovered in taking on a boyfriend on top of her commitment to him.

Closing her eyes as she turned on the jets to feel the water bubble and swirl around her in a most luxurious fashion, her mind drifted to the visual that she had come to savor of her husband kneeling before her as she dressed in sexy lingerie for her lover, an act that she was anxious to repeat and a thought that never failed to make her wet for reasons that she was still coming to terms with understanding herself…

Towering over him in her sky high heels that seemed all the more domineering because *he* had picked them out *for her*, she saw herself growing taller as he seemed to shrink beneath her – a testament to the powerful dynamic that was strangely developing between them as she began to enjoy the elements of *control* that her lover Marcus had hinted for her to use to enhance their own relationship.

Her mind then flipped once again to a new visual inspired by that very afternoon's latest developments as she envisioned her husband obediently doing chores around the house while she lay in their married bed upstairs with her lover. The thoughts grew naughtier as Kate pictured herself kneeling in front of the man with his thick cock in her mouth while her husband donned a classic maid's apron *and even a pair of black high heels* as he dusted the house while his chastity belt remained forever locked underneath.

As Kate finally found herself being vigorously fucked

while her husband looked on, tied to the bedposts with both his wrists and ankles spread and a shiny, red ballgag trapped in his mouth, that was when the woman finally gasped out loud as her caresses beneath the water eventually pushed her over the edge. After taking a few much needed moments to catch her breath, the happily satisfied woman eventually lifted herself back out of the tub and relaxingly toweled off before pulling a silky robe over her otherwise naked body and slipping into a pair of matching low-heeled sandals, then returned downstairs to the kitchen where she found her husband waiting for her at the table with two plates on the table and a chilled glass of wine nearby to accompany each…

"Well doesn't *this* look fabulous!" she gushed as she slid into the seat opposite him, eager to dig in after a long day of doing little to nothing. The two exchanged pleasant small talk as they ate, with Kate offering up many an impressed compliment about all the work that he had done to make their home more presentable throughout the day. When the conversation eventually turned to *the real subject* on both of their minds, Kate simply proposed, *"Let's talk about it after dinner…"* which she was surprised to see that he accepted without an ounce of resistance.

Once their plates had finally been emptied and she had thanked him kindly again for a great meal, Kate then suggested that he should clear the dishes and bring a fresh glass of wine up to the bedroom so that they could continue their discussion in a more comfortable setting. She next turned to leave him once more with his thoughts, grinning as she felt his eyes lock onto her silky legs that slipped out from beneath the robe with each step and wondering just how tantalizing that made him feel inside of that shiny, new prison of his.

Appearing at the doorway to their bedroom about ten minutes later, Andrew entered to find his wife reclined on the chaise lounger that sat in the corner of their room, facing the window. She smiled as he handed her the single glass of wine that he had brought with him at her request, then spoke up, "Why don't you take off your clothes and have a seat over here…"

A moment later, she added, "I still haven't had a good chance *to see it* yet."

Her husband quickly stripped down his clothes and piled them at the edge of the bed, admittedly feeling even more naked *wearing the belt* than he ever did without it, and after surveying the scene and taking note of his wife's graceful appearance, he eventually sat down by her feet at the end of the chaise.

"Does it hurt?" Kate asked unabashedly as she took a small sip from her glass, her eyes staring curiously at the steel device between his legs.

Andrew looked up, somewhat taken off guard by her question, though after a minute of processing soon responded, "No, well … *it depends.* Right now it's ok, but *the spikes* can get to be a little much at times…"

"At times like what???" his wife inquired, though the smirk that she almost perfectly held back still hinted that she already knew the answer.

"Ummmmm…" he stuttered. *"When I start getting* **aroused,** *they start to* **dig in…"**

"But I thought that you couldn't get hard inside of that thing…" Kate countered as if they were having a conversation about anything other than her husband's chastised member at that very moment.

"I can't … not fully," Andrew confirmed, adding, "…but if I

start on my way, *they hurt.*"

She could tell by the look on his face that he didn't know how to describe the sensation any better, despite having already experienced it *many times* in just the last few days.

"Interesting…" Kate purred as she took another sip from her wine.

"So tell me," she then asked with a curious tone to her voice, "what *exactly* has been arousing you the last couple of days since you've been wearing that???"

Andrew thought for a moment as he looked down at his locked crotch, then his eyes dropped back to her feet before he admitted, "Mostly you."

"Me?!" she repeated rather surprised. She considered his response herself for a moment before she just had to press, "Why … me … after all that I've done to you recently???"

Her husband's eyes wandered the room a while longer as she watched him ponder his response before finally looking right back at her and telling her, "I don't know … you've just been … *sexier lately.*"

Kate considered the response, then prompted, "Go on…" as she crossed her ankles in front of him.

"I mean – there's just something about you that's … *different,"* he continued. "You've had this new *aura* about you, and you never used to dress *like this* in the past…"

Kate smiled warmly as she looked down at him kneeling by her feet, then countered with an even more difficult question…

"Does it bother you that I'm sleeping with another man?"

"Yes," he replied almost instantly, to which Kate equally countered back, *"Why?"*

Andrew attempted to give the question some serious thought, but all the same appeared a little flabbergasted as he replied, "Because that's supposed to be *my job,* and because I thought that we were happy together."

"We *are* happy together," she told him with a comforting tone in her voice.

"But then why are you sleeping around?!" he argued, though he was quick to calm himself as he looked up at his wife and noted the lack of threatening appearance in her own stature as she simply listened and occasionally sipped from her glass, her toes seeming to sparkle in the moonlight coming in from the window.

"Don't you love me anymore?" he eventually came to sheepishly as his eyes dropped back to the floor.

"Of course I still love you," Kate comforted her husband without hesitation. "If I didn't love you, *I'd have just left you,* and clearly I'm still here…"

"So then why … *him?* Why *all of this???"* he asked, hinting down to the chastity belt.

With that Kate admittedly smirked as she thought of Marcus and glanced down at the device that she'd insisted he wear, reporting harshly, *"Because it's* **fun!"**

"We've been together for *fifteen years now,* and when this opportunity arose, I just thought that it might be fun to *experiment* a little. I'm not the same *pretty young thing* that I was when you met me, and it's been nice to remember what it's like to *feel sexy* all over again…"

"…even **you** *just admitted to that."*

Andrew's eyes continued to stay fixed on the floor in front of him as his wife continued.

"It's not about love, *even though I love being with him* … and even if I were to say that *in a way I kind of love him,* it's not in the same way that I love my partner who I've been with for the last decade and a half! *You're the one who I married* and *you're the one who I call my husband,* and nothing has happened in the last few months to change that."

Silence filled the room until eventually Andrew mumbled out the single word, "…*but…*"

"But … what do you want me to say?!" Kate said with a laugh. *"Yes, I enjoy fucking him! He's* **bigger than you,** *he's got* **so much more stamina than you,** *he's* **more passionate than you.** There's no question that when it comes to fucking, *you just can't even compete…"*

"But that doesn't mean that's **the only way** *that you can please me,"* she suggested hopefully as she noted the somber look on the man's face.

"What's that supposed to mean?" Andrew asked weakly as his eyes remained glued to the floor.

"Well, for starters, want to know one thing that I've learned about you just recently?" she asked in an attempt to turn the conversation up.

"What's that?"

"I've learned that I *really like* the look of you *at my feet,*" she told her husband with an earnest sincerity.

"Like right now, and even *that night,*" she expanded on her comment, "it makes me feel … *powerful, and sexy* … to have a man at my feet *to serve me.*"

"And you look *good* there – like that's *where you belong,* and it kind of *turns me on…*"

It was with her latest comment that Andrew's eyes rose back to his wife's feet, which were still crossed only inches away from his face and smelled sweetly of strawberries from her recent bath.

Sensing the up tick with a small smile, Kate uncrossed her feet and bent her knee to prop one up on the edge of the lounger in front of him, coyly asking, "You've been *noticing* my feet a lot more lately, haven't you?"

"It's ok…" she quickly added. "I know that you've always had a thing for shoes – it's *ironic* that I never wore those black ones that you wanted me to get until last weekend…"

She watched as she knew his mind flashed to her stocking-clad feet wrapped up in the sky high stiletto platforms, grinning herself at the thought of standing over him with such power, such authority, and then to command him to *kiss them* as if they were the only conduit to her that he deserved in that very moment in time.

"Is thinking about me **in those shoes** *one of the things that turns you on?"* Kate purred seductively as she wiggled her toes in front of her husband. *"I know it turned* **me** *on … watching you* **worship them** *before I went out to have* **my fun…"**

Andrew bit his lip and squirmed uncomfortably, but couldn't deny his wife's words and after 15 years, he knew that the look on his face was something that she could read like a book. He felt immensely attracted to her in that moment, and yet as he gazed up her long legs that were extended luxuriously out in front of him, his eyes fell short of the shimmering, silky red robe that just barely covered her most intimate parts … somehow once again as if *he wasn't allowed.*

"Why don't you get some lotion and you can rub my feet while we talk…" Kate suggested as she curiously examined his emotions from her perch. He simply nodded and stood up without a word to walk into the bathroom and retrieve a similarly scented bottle of the strawberry lotion that he knew she enjoyed in conjunction with the bath scents that she had used earlier, while Kate couldn't help but smile at the loving display of obedience that was unfolding right there in front of her, despite all that she had done to him in recent months.

As Andrew took his place once again at the end of his wife's chaise, he unwittingly looked up at her seemingly for her approval before he reached up and gently lifted the first of the two slip-on sandals from her feet that had apparently pedicured quite recently, though it was at that moment with a warm smile on Kate's face that he first took witness to a very special and very new piece of jewelry that he'd never noticed before…

Catching just enough moonlight from out the window to cast the tiniest of sparkles into his eyes, Andrew was drawn to the expensive-looking gold anklet that hung around her right ankle… the chain itself looking quite beautiful, yet the focal point – *at least in his eyes* – quite clearly was the discrete-looking charm in the shape of a small key that dangled freely within inches of his fingers as he removed the woman's shoe.

"You like my new anklet?" Kate asked him with a reserved smirk as his eyes remained locked on the gold chain. "Marcus bought it for me a couple of weeks ago, but told me that I couldn't wear it *until its accessory was ready*. To answer the question that I'm sure is looming in your head – **yes, that's the key to your chastity belt.**"

She wiggled her toes playfully as his stare continued until she finally had to jilt him back into the present as she snapped her fingers, *"Come on – lotion?"*

Andrew set his wife's shoe to the side and squeezed a small amount of the scented lotion into his hand before reaching out and caressing it into the sole of Kate's foot.

"Mmmmm – *that feels good…"* she quietly moaned, chuckling under her breath, *"…see – you're still good for something…"*

He did his best to focus on his wife's feet, taking a much more slow and sensual focus than usual as he keyed into her reactions and paid particular attention to the stiffest of areas, though it was no secret that his eyes continued to wander back to the anklet that dangled freely from his wife's ankle – just inches above where his fingers stopped their work – until finally he heard her ask him with a somewhat sarcastic tone.

"Does it just drive you crazy to see your key **right there** *and not be able to do anything about it???"*

The chastised man froze for a second, then resumed his efforts with his eyes now fixated solely on the woman's toes as he meekly replied back, "You don't seem to be very interested in my cock right now anyways…"

Kate laughed, then took a slow drink of her wine before replying.

"Again - dick, not cock, honey … but that's not *entirely* true. I'm very interested in your dick *right where it is right now* – I just don't have any *sexual desire* for it at the moment!"

She smiled as she looked down her legs at him, fishing for his response as she read the embarrassed expression on his face with an unexpected hint of glee. He focused on her foot, working the smooth cream in between her brightly-painted toes before muttering another response – "I guess it doesn't matter if I'm locked up or not then…"

Albeit the circumstances were a bit different than usual, the brunette had experienced her husband's *poor me attitude* far too many times and in this case had no intention of letting it dampen her mood.

"So are you agreeing that it should be locked up if I have no desire to make use of it???" she quipped with a certain chime to her voice that she knew ground him to the core with just the intended effect. Glancing up at his wife's face for the briefest moment without a word before removing her other shoe and continuing his focus at her feet, Kate summarized their *conversation* with a playful giggle as she spoke to no one in particular, "You know, it pleases me to see you coming around on the idea so quickly. That's going to make this a lot easier…"

The exercise went on for a few minutes longer in silence as Kate enjoying simply watching her husband focus on her feet while Andrew fought internally with all that was taking place around him, still uncomfortable with the thought of his wife with another man, yet strangely centered on the task before him, and admittedly even the slightest bit *aroused* inside of his steel chastity belt through the limited interaction that he had been allowed at his wife's feet.

"I was really pleased with everything that you did around the house today, by the way…" she spoke randomly in a concerted effort to break the silence between them.

Andrew replied with a simple, "Thank you…" as he looked up at his wife with a small smile, inside grateful that she had noticed his effort as he rubbed his thumbs deep into her soles.

"So tell me," she continued, *"what made you do it?"*

"What do you mean?" he asked in what felt like his first not nervous reply simply from a state of confusion.

"Why did you choose to spend your day doing the things that you did?" Kate clarified astutely. "Surely with everything that's happened lately, you would have every right to *just be pissed off at me* and lay around watching TV all day … *especially when I spent all day working on my tan!"*

"I'm just curious – *what made you choose to spend your day off doing chores instead???"*

He thought for a moment, then stopped and looked up at his wife from the floor and gently told her, *"To make you happy…"*

Kate paused as she watched her husband go back to work before prompting him, "Elaborate…"

Andrew stopped the long foot massage again, put his hands in his lap, and looked up at Kate once more as he tried to explain, "I thought that maybe *all of this* was because *you were mad at me* about something, so I wanted to do something to try and make it better…"

"Oh, dear…" she comforted him as she took another small sip from her glass, "you didn't do anything to make me mad, *but you* **did** *please me with your efforts around the house today – that made me* **very happy."**

"…I see that you even had *my new dress and lingerie* dry cleaned…"

He bit his lip as he stared downward, then replied meekly with a shrug, "It needed to get done. They were dirty, and I figured that you'd want to wear them again at some point…"

Kate smiled.

"You did, did you???"

With that, the two were interrupted as Kate's phone began to ring from its place beside her on the chaise. Unsure of what else to do besides simply resume what he had been doing earlier, Andrew took his wife's by now quite tender feet in his hands once more as she began to talk, though it didn't take long for him to piece together who was on the other end of the phone…

"Hey, baby – it's so good to hear from you. I figured you must be pretty swamped on your business trip because you hadn't called yet!"

"Things are good … in fact, we were actually talking about that **right now** *while he treats me to a nice, little foot rub…"*

"Of course he's still wearing it! Hardly any complaints at all. He even did all sorts of stuff for me around the house without a single complaint, including getting my new outfit from last weekend all cleaned up for me…"

"Yup!"

"Mmmmmm – that does sound nice … kind of makes me wish that

I was **there to share it with you…"**

"Teeheehee! Actually, **I've got an idea!** *Hold on for a minute…"*

Holding the phone down to her chest, Kate finally looked back at her husband who was still sitting at her feet quite anxiously.

"Andrew…"

"Do you want me to go and give you two some privacy?" he asked in a mopey tone.

"Nope!" she chimed back without missing a beat. "I want you to go to the closet and bring back *those shoes* of mine that you like. You missed out on the chance to help me put them on last time – let's see if you can avoid making the same again…"

Andrew looked back at his wife confused after just listening to her randomly flirting with the subject of her affair, but for some reason knew better than to question it as he lifted himself up to his feet and disappeared into the closet, only to return a few seconds later carrying the same strappy, black platform heels that he had retrieved for his wife a few days prior, though he still wasn't quite sure of her intent this go around on account of what *he did* overhear about her lover being out of town on business at the moment.

Pointing him with a single finger to return to his place at her feet, Kate chimed with a proud grin on her face as she held her phone off to the side to address him, *"Now Andrew, you impressed me* **so much** *this afternoon by taking the initiative to get my dress cleaned, I'm going to let you enjoy* **cleaning my heels** *for the next few minutes while I* **chat with my friend here** *on the phone!"*

"Do be sure to **pay extra attention** *to the soles and the heels, as I was on my feet in them a lot that night … at least until, well,* **you know…"**

Andrew blushed as he dropped his focus back to his wife's feet before taking a seat once again at the end of the chaise, this time feeling a little further from her than earlier as he began to fit the strappy stilettos around her beautiful feet while she returned to her conversation as if he couldn't even hear her.

"Sorry about that — just had to give a little direction to get things underway here. So tell me … **how much have you missed me?"**

Her husband's eyes fixated on the shiny, gold key hanging from her ankle, now more symbolic than ever as he seemed to be willingly participating in her little charade as he carefully buckled the numerous straps around her feet, admittedly feeling himself growing a bit aroused underneath his belt despite all of the undertones that this new fantasy world that had sprouted up around him seemed to suggest in a myriad of not-so-subtle ways.

"That sounds nice…" he heard Kate purr into the phone while he did his best to remain focused on her shoes as he continued to fit the second high heel to her other foot, his mind transported away as his fetish was overwhelmed by the divine scent of leather melding with her new strawberry-scented aura just before his face.

"Oh god, what I wouldn't do for your touch right now…" she moaned as she adjusted her position on the couch, spreading her legs ever so slightly as he watched her free hand out of the corner of his eye wander up underneath her robe to toy with her nipples.

It didn't seem right to watch, **even if she was his own married wife,** and so closing his eyes, Andrew followed the woman's orders to the tee as he leaned in and began to run his tongue up and down the soles of the platform heels in his most submissive display yet, all the while Kate's side of the dialog between her and her lover seemed to grow more and more risqué as she touched herself intimately and without remorse…

"I'd love to feel you between my lips, straddling my head as I get you ready…"

"Inside me deep, nice and slow to get my juices flowing…"

"I can almost taste you as you suddenly start **ramming into me** *harder and harder!"*

Kate grinned as she looked down her legs to see Andrew so obediently at work on her shoes before she flipped her robe open and began touching herself much aggressively at her boyfriend's instructions, first pulling at her nipples that by then were quite erect and then finally bringing her hand south to massage her clit as the man's erotic narration from over the phone began to push her to climax.

"Oh, fuck me, Sir – **I'm yours!"** Andrew heard his wife cry out as he did his best to keep his lips wrapped around the stiletto heel of her right shoe while she flailed about with

passion on the chaise in their master bedroom. Though his penis began to ache against the sharp spines that cradled it inside the belt, he cuckolded man managed to keep his eyes welded tightly shut as he tasted the leather spike on his tongue and between his lips until he finally witnessed in the flesh his wife being brought to orgasm by the work of another right in front of him…

"Oh … that was **wonderful…"** she moaned warmly after the initial scream had subsided and the pulsating within her body was beginning to dissipate. The two made pillow talk for a few minutes longer as the married woman drifted back to Earth until it was finally time to say their goodbyes, all the while her husband continued worshipping her heels without interruption, much to his wife's pleasure.

"That was fun – so when are you going to be back so that we can do it in person next time???"

"Grrrrr … that sounds like **so long!"**

"Teeheehee!" she giggled like a schoolgirl, crossing her legs and forcing her husband to change his position once again. *"I just want your cock inside of me …* **my pussy craves you!!!"**

After another minute of playful banter, Kate finally hung up the phone and returned her attention at last to subservient man suckling at her feet. Thoroughly enjoying the sight as she looked down at her stiletto-clad feet and admired Andrew giving his all to the soles of the very shoes that she had flaunted in his face a few days prior, she amusingly activated the camera on her phone and quickly took several shots of him in all of his glory – *nude with his chastity belt clearly in frame, reverently with his scandalous wife's sexy shoes at his lips…*

Before finally giving him permission to cease and help her get ready for bed, she just couldn't help herself in sending a couple of her prime shots back to Marcus as he was ready to retire himself in his hotel room on the other side of the country.

"Baby, I want you to see what just happened…" she captioned the two photos of her husband at his most humble, with them ironically also being the first that he'd ever seen of her legally bound partner.

"He's learning fast," he commented back a few moments later.

"Yes, yes he is…" was her last text reply back before turning back to see her husband in a surprisingly different light that she wouldn't have expected, but had a feeling she was rather going to enjoy.

* * * * * * * * *

The next few days in the Jones household were much less tense between the couple as they began to more openly explore this new lifestyle that Kate had been turned on to. Although his days still very much took some getting used to as he continued to wear the steel chastity belt as prescribed 24x7, through a means of extra work around the house and nightly foot rubs when he returned home, Andrew was at least granted a hint of relief as his wife found the sympathy to retract the spikes inside of the belt … at least for the time being…

Conversations pushed forward as well during each of their nightly sessions, with Andrew focusing on her feet while they talked about what her new relationship meant in comparison to their own as he seemed to reluctantly drift into a place where he almost seemed that he might be able to *be comfortable* with the whole affair.

At the end of each night before he went to sleep and again the next morning before he left for work, Kate began a ritual of expecting him to *kiss her feet* prior to his departure – more affectionately at times and occasionally limited to only her big toe when she was feeling feisty. Although she hadn't replayed another session where she watched her husband so passionately worshipping her shoes because there was a part of her that wished to reserve such a vivid display for more special occasions, she couldn't deny that she grew a bit fonder of her husband's time at her feet with every day that passed.

Another week had nearly gone by when Andrew found himself with most of his work caught up at the office when his phone vibrated with a text message from his wife…

"Need you to stop and pick up a package for me on your way home from work."

"No problem," he quickly replied. "What is it?"

"Not really sure, but the address is 647 Faraday Street. Any idea when you're heading home???"

The two exchanged messages for a few more iterations

before Andrew finally told her that he had to get back to work, although in reality he had actually planned on sneaking out early to surprise her. After first stopping off to pick up a bottle of wine for dinner and a nice bouquet of flowers for his dominating bride, he then punched the address that she had given him into his GPS and drove another 10 miles out of his way to pick up her mystery package, though when the device finally announced that he had reached his destination, looking up at the sign over the door left his imagination reeling, wondering what he could possibly be picking up for her in that particular part of town.

Hank's House of Flesh – the sign read as he put his car into park and took a quick look around the parking lot to survey the area before getting out. Thankfully it was still only mid-afternoon and very much light out, so Andrew felt relatively safe as he got out of his car and made his way across the empty parking lot to the single, windowless door with a smaller version of the company's logo tacked to the front…

Upon walking inside, he found himself in what appeared to be a typical adult toy store with rows upon rows of DVDs immediately inside and various other sections of magazines and bachelorette novelties off in the distance. His eyes darted confusingly around the empty store until a feminine voice from behind the counter beside him caught his attention, "Hey there! We normally don't get many customers this time of day – is there something that I can help you with?"

Andrew turned to see that the origin of the voice was a small, blonde girl with her hair pulled back in a ponytail, flipping the pages of a magazine while she sat seemingly bored at the counter.

"Oh, ummmm," he stumbled as he turned towards the counter, "I'm supposed to pick up a package for my wife … but I'm wondering if maybe she gave me the wrong address…"

The blonde shrugged off his nervousness and asked him, "The wife, huh? What's the name???"

"Jones? Katherine Jones."

"Nope – you're in the right place!" she chimed back without a glance at any of the paperwork or the computer nearby. "I spoke with your wife earlier to tell her that it was ready

… Hank poured it yesterday and it should've had plenty of time to cure overnight…"

Andrew pondered deeply the various terms that the girl had thrown out while she temporarily disappeared into the back, returning a few moments later with a white cardboard box which she placed in front of him on the counter before stepping back around.

"It actually turned out *really nice,*" the girl said as she took her seat back on the stool behind the counter before spinning the box in her direction and flipping open the tabs to reveal its contents. "Plus as you'll see, the model that we got was of a really good quality, so there were all sorts of veins and textures that came through in the final mold that we don't normally see when somebody just tries to do it themselves…"

His bewildered look persisted as Andrew had not the faintest idea what the girl was talking about until finally she spun the box back around and revealed to him *the package* that he had been sent to pick up for his wife – *a very large,* **very realistic dildo** *that seemed to take up the lion's share of the box and made him* **instantly** *feel a bit smaller in his cage as he stood there wide-eyed as the girl continued her sales pitch.*

"We mold them with a special thermal plastic that's very realistic, *both in touch and in weight* – you'll see when you pick it up…" she explained as she ushered Andrew to take the phallus from its display box in his own hands. He'd never actually held a dildo before, but she was definitely accurate in that the fake cock felt surprisingly like a real one … *aside from his own which felt exceptionally cold and small at the moment.*

Also much *unlike* his own, this cock seemed considerably larger, to the point where as he eyed its length the salesgirl eventually read his mind and reported proudly, "It's a solid 8-1/2" long – just as you had requested!"

It took him another few moments of gawking at the dildo's sheer size in comparison before he finally circled back to her comments and corrected her, *"Oh, no -* ***I*** *didn't request this…"* with the realistic dildo still in his hands.

The girl looked at him confused, then turned over to the computer and punched a few buttons before turning back with an apologetic look on her face…

"Oh, I'm sorry – *you're not Mr. Powers.* You're Mr. Jones … *the husband*, aren't you? My mistake – so sorry for the confusion!"

Andrew felt a lump in his throat as he carefully set the dildo back into its box and began to put the pieces together in his head as he quickly thanked the girl for her time and retreated back to his car, carrying the box awkwardly under one arm as his eyes scanned the parking lot once again to confirm that he was alone as he approached his vehicle.

Setting the box down in the passenger seat next to his flowers and wine, he sat there in contemplation for a moment before surprisingly he found himself reaching back to look inside of the box once more, taken aback by what he had a feeling the rubber phallus represented before eventually closing it up once again and driving home again in complete silence.

Walking in the door with both arms full as he carried his things from work, along with the flowers, the wine, *and of course,* **the box,** Andrew found himself greeted quite eagerly by Kate as she took the box from only from his hands and rushed into the kitchen to open it.

"Is that what I think it is???" he asked as he followed her in after kicking off his shoes by the door.

"I have *no idea* what it is — *he didn't tell me!*" she confessed with a giggle as she set the box down on the counter and ogled it like a kid on Christmas morning, looking up in excitement at her husband as he placed the wine in the fridge before then ceremoniously flipped up the cardboard flap, with her jaw dropping as she saw the box's contents herself for the very first time…

"No shit!" Kate exclaimed as she took the cock from its resting place and held it in marvel out in front of her, examining it in awe as her husband stood awkwardly off to the side. "It's *just like* the real thing…" she spoke out loud as she held the dildo curiously in her hands, admiring the large vein that ran down the top and even the sizable balls that seemed to provide a sturdy base to hold the toy by.

Looking up and sensing her husband's unease, Kate put the dildo back down and took the flowers from him, setting them in the sink as she told him, "These are pretty – thank you! Now *drop your pants … I want to show you something…"*

Andrew felt himself begin to sink back into the role that he had been growing more and more accustomed to over the past week as without question he unbuckled his belt and dropped both his trousers and his underwear right there in the middle of their kitchen while Kate bent down and plucked the key from her anklet as she stood barefoot in front of him. Then crouching down at his groin level, his wife proceeded to insert her key into the locking mechanism of the belt for the first time since he'd donned it and a few seconds later, he was looking at his dick once more … though by now it seemed like only a fraction of its former self after having been crammed inside of the steel contraption for nearly 10 days.

"Hands behind your back!" she commanded unexpectedly as she walked back over to her new gift and retrieved the phallus from the box that he had brought home for her. Caressing its length and girth with her fingers much more seductively this time, Kate slowly walked over to where her husband stood nervously and reported to him bluntly, **"This …** *is what pleases me these days…"* then pointing down to his own dick and swatting it gently with the back of her hand, added, **"That …** *does not…"*

Then taking the 8-1/2" artificial cock and holding it at his crotch where his own was quickly beginning to grow, she laughed as she compared the two in size side-by-side, jeering him with a sweet sarcasm in her voice, *"Sorry, baby, but* **you just don't stack up** *anymore…"*

Andrew looked his dominant wife in the eye as his erection grew with every word, yet still paled in comparison to the replicate of *Marcus's cock* that she held beside it.

"You know," she continued to taunt him as she paced back and forth, toying with the impressive dildo in her hands, "it's always seemed like there was *something* missing in the bedroom between us … *but now that I can see the comparison with my very own eyes,* **the answer** is pretty clear to see!"

Sliding over to her husband with her back to him as she pressed up against him – *and his erect cock* – while she reached back and looked at him over her shoulders, Kate purred provocatively into his ear, *"I want a cock like Marcus's, honey … I* **need** *a cock like Marcus's…"*

Andrew clenched his wrists behind his back in agony as the incredible woman's as seemed to tease him perfectly through her skirt. Without knowing what he was saying, he simply replied, *"I know…"* as he looked down into the deep brown eyes that seemed to twist the knife deeper with every flutter.

"Mmmmmm…" she moaned as she pushed her body backwards into him even harder.

"So are you saying that **it's ok** *for me to* **be fulfilled** *by Marcus???"*

"Is it **ok** *for me to* **take his big, thick cock** *because yours is* **much too small???"**

"And is it **ok** *for me to* **keep you all locked up** *while my* **boyfriend** **expertly** *fucks me over and over again???"*

Although he wanted anything just to touch her, Andrew whimpered as he tried to grind himself into his wife's ass as she pulled away and then turned around to face him. Inching closer, he ached merely to touch her, and he thought for a brief moment that he might have his chance as she leaned forward as if to kiss him … but instead, just before their lips were to touch, Andrew found himself with an up close and personal view as just inches from his lips, his wife wantonly parted her own and invited the dildo inside … twirling her tongue over the head as she gave it a few practice strokes before thoroughly blowing his mind by suddenly taking the 8-1/2" cock in her mouth fully in her mouth up to the balls before removing it a moment later with a sexy wink and a sultry smile on her pouty lips that had never given Andrew's penis nearly the same level of enthusiasm.

"I'm sure that you'd like to see more…" Kate told her husband coyly as she danced back over to the box and carefully stowed it away for later use, *"but that's a bit private, and you just haven't earned* **that** *yet…"*

Then scooping a free ice cube out of her nearby drink just as she'd been instructed, the woman wasted no time shocking Andrew's dick back to its non-erect size and then frankly tucking it back inside of its chamber with little commentary other than the growing smirk on her face, though just before telling him to pull his pants up once again, Kate did click the spikes back into position #2 which elicited a sharp wince from their victim as she stood up before him.

"Now I want to be clear about those," Kate told her husband as she patted him just gently enough on the outside of the belt to stir his dick into their range, "you haven't done anything *wrong,* per se. In fact, I've been rather *pleased* with your performance these last couple of days and seeing your renewed focus on … *me!"*

She motioned over towards the flowers, then turned her attention back to him and continued to massage the front side of his chastity belt.

"But what you have to understand is that the spikes are really there for *two purposes* – the first purpose is for *punishment,* for when you misbehave or you do something that displeases me, and the second reason is for *suffering* … the suffering is really for *whatever I want it to be.* Right now the reason that I want you to *suffer* is because you're incapable of pleasing me *yourself* … that's why *you're in this belt,* and why *I'm going to go upstairs and fuck my boyfriend's new dildo."*

"When I come back down, I'll most likely disengage them and we can both share in the lovely dinner that you're about to create for us," she continued with a strong tone in her voice. "But in the meantime, while you're down here chopping and frying, and I'm up there *moaning and bucking against this* **perfect replica** *of my lover's cock* … I want that to *sting* a little bit, *do you understand me?"*

"Yes, ma'am," Andrew spit out without a second thought, much to his wife's delight, though she didn't show any signs of it as she kept her eyes dead locked on her own.

"Good," she simply replied curtly. "So get down on the floor and *show me* that you understand…"

Andrew instantly dropped to the floor and quickly brought his lips within an inch of his commanding wife's foot, but was soon intercepted as she interjected one last note into her direction.

"Not the big one this time," she chimed. "That doesn't seem quite … *appropriate.*"

"No, this time I want you to kiss **only my little toe** … *you know,* **little – just like your tiny, little dick…"**

Andrew carefully shifted his lips to just barely touch the freshly painted, sparkling red nail on her little toe, and only held it in place for what felt like half a second before Kate stepped away and left him staring at the tile floor with his pants still wrapped around his ankles.

"I'm going to go upstairs for a while and try out my new present!" she called out to him in a demeanor polar opposite to that which had just transpired. "Thanks again for picking it up for me, sweetie – I'll be down for dinner in about an hour…"

Kate had already run up the stairs and closed the bedroom door behind her by the time that her husband had come back to his senses and lifted himself back off the floor, though she took extra care *not* to hold back on her enthusiasm as she gave the ultra-realistic dildo the workout that could only be met by the real thing, this time riding a brand new high as she also imagined those tiny spikes inside of her husband's chastity belt digging into his dick with every moan of excitement and entertaining the idea for the very first time that he was, in fact, somehow *suffering for her.*

* * * * * * * * *

"Can you come upstairs when you have a minute?" Kate called down to her husband as she finished straightening her hair in front of the mirror. "I've got something that I want to tell you before I head out…"

Andrew already knew of his wife's plans for the evening because after making nightly use of her new gift, she was exceptionally giddy about Marcus's return home from his business trip and had been very much looking forward to sharing a drink with him … *along with all of the rest that they both knew came with it.*

Stepping into the bedroom a few minutes later to find her

once again preparing herself for a night out, he noted that this evening's attire was considerably more casual than their last adventure, with her iconic, tight leather dress replaced by a simple, flowing sundress in a myriad of bright colors and paired with a moderate, high heeled wedge that she'd already slipped onto her feet.

"Hey, dear," she greeted him with a warm smile of a much different tone after all of the progress that the two had made together during the past week. "If you can just take off your clothes and leave them in the hamper, I'll be ready in *just a minute…*"

The request was getting to be common place around their house, in that Andrew no longer hesitated as he did as he was told and removed his clothing while he waited, leaving nothing behind except for the shiny, steel belt between his legs that he didn't have the ability to take off anyways.

A short while later, Kate emerged from the bathroom and was delighted to see her husband standing near the bed waiting for her, nude save for his chastity belt just like she had requested and also holding his hands behind his back – a position that she most definitely *didn't request,* yet she enjoyed the perspective and thought that it fit what was about to take place just the same.

"So…" she began as she rummaged through her purse momentarily before turning her attention back to Andrew, "…what I wanted to tell you is that I've been *immensely happy* with how you've *improved* over the last couple of weeks. I know that you've been locked inside that belt for something like *two weeks now,* and I'm sure that it must be frustrating to *not cum* for such an extended period of time…"

"…*especially when* **I've** *been doing quite the opposite!*"

Andrew blushed and looked down at the floor as his wife hinted at the true-to-life-sized dildo that was seemingly *on display* nearby on her nightstand.

She paced around to face him as she jingled the key to his belt between her fingers, slowly tracing her free hand around his bound crotch while she continued…

"I've been doing a lot of *research* online lately about all of this, and some people say that it's not good for a man to go *too long* without an orgasm. They listed a number of ways that a woman *in my position* can deal with this sort of thing, and so I've decided to show you *a bit of mercy* this evening before I go out and show you the type of orgasm that I'm going to permit *you* to have while you're otherwise locked up in that belt for me. *How does that sound???"*

Andrew looked back up to meet her eyes with a glimmer of enthusiasm as he professed, *"That sounds* **wonderful,** *ma'am!"*

Kate smiled as he called her *ma'am* so submissively once again.

"Well I'm glad that you're glad!" she confirmed, further explaining, "…but if we're going to do this, we're going to do it *my way…"*

He simply nodded in reply, as if anything else at that point was even an option.

Kate stepped back over to the vanity and retrieved a couple of items that had been hidden behind her purse, collecting them both with a sly grin on her face as she returned to her husband's side, albeit this time from behind as she whispered softly into his ear…

"A few rules for how our little game shall be played here,"

she began as she first took the satin pillowcase that she had folded into the shape of a blindfold and cinched it softly, but firmly around his head.

"No sight…"

She then surprised him as she took his wrists and ratcheted a very real pair of handcuffs around them, now held even more securely behind his back.

"No touch…"

She finally came back around to his front and knelt down to release the belt that was around his waist, carefully loosening the mechanism so as to not pinch anything as his tiny dick popped free and already began to grow before her own eyes once again as she temporarily set his chastity belt in its entirety off to the side.

"And no cumming without permission…"

"What that means," she elaborated with a sly grin that she was clearly enjoying, despite her one and only audience being completely blind to her performance, "is that when you think you're ready to cum, *you're to ask me if you're allowed to cum first.*"

"You'll say, **'Miss Jones, may I cum?'"**

"And it's as simple as that – if I say *yes,* you're free to follow through with *all of what has been pent up for nearly two weeks now,* but when I say *no* … **don't you dare…"**

"Do you understand the rules of our little game here, Andrew???" Kate asked condescendingly as she swelled with all of the power that she had somehow gained from this man who she had once considered to be her loving equal.

"Yes, ma'am – I understand," he immediately replied without hesitation as he spread his legs while his dick stood already at half mast.

"Now let's see how long you last…" Kate then giggled as she nonchalantly reached down and took a firm hold of her husband's member, in awe of his every reaction as she wondered what was going through his head at that very moment amidst the sea of dominant changes that were all taking place around him so fast. The night before, he had spent several hours at her request reorganizing and cleaning her entire shoe collection, and a about a week prior he had sucked on her heels while she flirted – *and eventually came to the sounds of her lover's voice* – over the phone.

He seemed to be slipping further and further beneath her feet with every effort, and even as she slowly massaged his dick with her hand right then and there, she felt a new role developing above him as she considered the hands *that would be touching* **her** a matter of hours from then!

"How does that feel, my little cuckold?" she asked him caustically, noticing a brief chill as she caught herself referring to him by *the actual word* for the very first time.

Andrew first just moaned as he stood there before her, blind and incapacitated with his dick his only connection to the outside world, until finally grunting, "It feels good…"

"It feels good, **what?!"** she challenged, stopping her gentle strokes and instead taking his penis between her nails in a manner that very sharply reminded him of the chastity spikes that taunted him on a regular basis.

"Oh, ummmm – *I'm sorry, ma'am … Miss Jones …* **I'm not sure what I'm supposed to call you…"** he admitted as he winced from the pain of his wife's fingernails.

Kate relaxed her grip and replied, "You can call me either

… for now…" before slowly resuming her stroking once again and then eventually adding in the narration that she was quickly growing more fond of incorporating into *her sessions* spent with him…

"I'll bet it **feels good** *to be touched, even just for a brief moment, doesn't it? I know that* ***I*** *can't wait to be touched* **by a real man** *later on tonight!"*

"You know that I just can't wait to feel myself in his strong arms once again…"

"And feel his tongue sensuously tango with mine…"

"And then feel him push my panties to the side when we finally slip off together and he plunges his cock inside of me because we just can't hold it back anymore…"

"Miss Jones, may I cum?" Andrew croaked out, leading his wife to immediately release her grip on his dick as she pulled her hand back and told him, *"No!"* before taking notice of his shaking body and giggling at what he had become.

"Does that **turn you on???"** she taunted, whispering into his ear as she gave his penis a chance to cool down. *"Does*

it **turn you on** *that* **it turns your wife on,** *being so blatantly unfaithful to you???"*

"You know, most men **would leave a wife** *who insisted that her husband's own dick* **wasn't satisfying enough** *for her … but this is* **so much** *more fun, honey!"*

With a coy grin that she almost wished he could witness with his own eyes, she took his dick in her hand once again as she continued…

"Does it help **to visualize** *a bit more now that you've seen a replica of his actual cock … and you're able to see* **with your very own eyes** *just how short you fall in comparison to him?"*

Kate took her teetering husband off guard when she suddenly leaned in and sucked one of his nipples into her mouth, taking it between her teeth before biting down and causing him to shout out in pain, *"Oh god!"*

She laughed as she released her teeth and pulled back, the rhythm in her hand increasing nonetheless.

"Not god … **goddess…"** she corrected him in laughter.

"Goddess, may I cum?!" he groaned again, reluctantly

resulting in yet another release as Kate this time took a step back and briefly pondered *Goddess* as her new title before resuming her taunting streak with even more vigor than ever.

"No! Why do **you** *deserve to cum when you're not even capable of* **making me cum?!"**

"Maybe I should just lock you back up and be on my way … I certainly don't want to keep Marcus waiting **for this…"**

She could tell by her husband's breathing that he was nearly spent as she watched him shudder as she ran a single finger from the tip down to the base of his sorely erect penis that seemed to just be begging to be touched. Even the slightest grazing of her nails against the tender flesh made him pout beneath his blindfold, and she could tell that he was *just shy* of begging for the release that she had been denying him.

"Remember back when **you used to be allowed to fuck me?"** she jeered as she just barely touched the head of his cock with her fingertips.

"Back before I started sneaking off with Dr. Powers at work for a

little fun after change of shift???"

"Well," she grunted as she felt herself getting aroused by her own narration as well, *"the truth of the matter is … when you used to fuck me back then … on our anniversary, or on your birthday, or on a random Saturday night???* **I couldn't even feel it!"**

Kate grabbed a hold of Andrew's dick and began to jerk him off aggressively.

"I didn't even know what a real cock felt like **until I felt Marcus's pounding** *into my pussy!"*

"I kind of wish that he was here **right now,** *just so* **my cuckolded husband** *could hear the sounds that his wife makes* **when she's getting fucked by a real man…"**

"MISS JONES, MAY I PLEASE CUM?!?!?!" Andrew moaned frantically as he felt himself beginning to lose control as everything around him, from his wife's touch to her taunts to even his bondage all finally got the best of him and he was ready to cum after a long and hard two weeks of being locked up tight in chastity.

"Yes, you may…" Kate said with a laugh in her voice as she

suddenly released her grasp on her husband's dick one last time and watched with great amusement as he thrust frantically at the air, desperately in search of the last ounce of stimulation that he needed until he finally heard his wife start to cackle after just the slightest drop of fluid seeped out of his abused penis. Andrew fought in vain against the handcuffs behind his back, but found no luck until he eventually just broke out in protest…

"I thought you said that I could cum!"

His wife's laughter continued as she unknowingly took a couple of snapshots with her phone of her husband's predicament before volleying back, "I did say that you could cum, *so what are you waiting for?!"*

He whimpered as he thrust at the air again, complaining, "But I need your help! Why did you stop?!"

Kate grinned, overwhelmed with joy that her plan had worked exactly as she had read about it online before finally explaining, "You've just experienced your first *ruined orgasm,* honey! *That's* the type of orgasm that you're permitted to have as long as *I* have you locked in chastity…"

"Kate, come on!" he continued to whine as she simply stood to the side and watched his erection slowly subside due to the lack of stimulation. "You promised…"

"You know, that whining is **so sexy,** *but I think it's about time that I got on my way!"* she taunted her husband before giving him a few surprisingly effective swats on his bare ass that seemed to reduce his size small enough that she could slip it back inside of its cage with little effort. Though his whimpers turned to something a little more serious once the belt was finally back in place and Kate proceeded to re-engage the spikes, clicking them first to a familiar level, then two notches beyond in response to his pathetic display in just the past couple of minutes…

Standing back in front of him, with his eyes still blinded by the satin pillowcase tied around his head, Kate dug her fingernails into both of his nipples simultaneously as she pulled him close and told him, *"I want you to know that* **part of those spikes** *is because I'm going out with my lover, and* **the other part** *is on account of the whining.* **Be a better play toy for me next time and it won't hurt this bad again…"**

She then released his nipples and instead took him by the ear as she forced him down on his knees and said, "Now tell your cuckoldress goodbye in the only way that you know how…"

Kate looked in the mirror to see herself *glowing* as Andrew slowly inched himself the rest of the way down to the floor with his wrists still cuffed behind him, then fished around for his wife's feet until he was able to kiss the cork sandals goodbye with only the brief memory from earlier as to what they actually even looked like.

"I'm not sure what time I'll be home … *you understand,"* she joked to herself, "but in the meantime, if you want to get out of those cuffs, I'm going to leave the keys downstairs somewhere for you to find. Call it a little … *game* that I read about online … *there is* **all sorts of stuff** *like this out there once you know where to look!"*

"Anyways, you should be able to get that blindfold off without *too much* effort. Then once you've found the keys, you're free to do whatever you wish with the rest of your evening."

Her purse in one hand and the handcuff keys in the other, she couldn't help but nudge him a couple of times with her high heels as she walked past, dancing down the stairs with a level of confidence and sex appeal that she hadn't felt in all her life, reaching the front door with a spring in her step before Andrew even had a chance to attempt to get back up on his knees again with the cuffs seriously starting to take their toll.

Taking a quick gander around the family room for an out of the way location to stow his keys, Kate played back the incredible exchange that had just occurred and applauded herself for lording her control over him to amazing, new heights. Giggling to herself as she took a surprising bit of pleasure in his suffering both through her game as well as the ongoing taunts of her naughty night yet to come, then in one final show of authority as she looked around and no one place in particular in the room jumped out at her, Kate merely *dropped the handcuff keys into her own purse* with a satisfied smirk before slinging it over her shoulder and calling out, **"Happy hunting, dear!"** before closing the door triumphantly behind her…

Her New Cuckold ...Transformed

Her New Cuckold ... Transformed

"
So how's your little *subby hubby* taking to his new role around the house???" Veronica asked Kate with a grin as the two sat alone eating their lunches in the break room at the hospital where they worked.

Kate snickered, pausing for a moment as her eyes darted around the room before she allowed herself to speak freely.

"You know, he's actually accepting it all *a lot better* than I ever would've expected!" she said with a laugh as she took another bite of the pasta that he'd prepared for her the night before. *"A lot better..."*

"Good!" her younger co-worker chimed with a bubbly grin as her mind flashed back to a couple of months prior when she had lent her services to first introduce Kate's husband to the world of chastity while she and her lover were out enjoying a night on the town. "If you ask me, *every woman* should have two men in her life – one to do all of the work and to wait on her hand and foot, and another *much more ravishing fellow* to have her fun with!"

"You may be right," Kate giggled along with her as the thought of her much more endowed lover … *the doctor* … made her slightly blush as she considered their latest rendezvous just the other night.

"I'm glad to see that he's been so willing to … *adjust* … to this new change to our lifestyle," she added as she daintily picked at her vegetables. "It certainly has made things … *easier* … for me."

Never one to shy away from even the most provocative of discussion topics, Veronica pressed on, "Well I should hope so! It's been what – over two months now? He should be doing almost *all* of the chores around the house at this point, isn't he???"

"Oh, he's getting there!" Kate smiled. "He's got most of the big stuff down by now – dishes, laundry, vacuuming … he spends a lot of time *reorganizing my closet for me* these days, probably because he fantasizes about the different outfits that Marcus has been buying for me."

"Does he cook?" Veronica asked curiously as she peered over into the plastic dish that Kate was eating from.

"Actually, he does," she replied, "and he's been getting surprisingly good at it as of late, too! We try to make an evening of it a couple of times a week on the nights that I'm home … he cooks something up and pours a bottle of wine, and then afterwards I'll put him to work either rubbing my feet or giving me a massage while I…"

Veronica grinned.

"So why haven't you had me over for dinner yet?! I kind of think that **you owe it to me** *after all of the* **groundwork** *that I laid for you that night!"* she jeered playfully.

"And besides, Andrew seemed like he was *awfully fun to tease* the last time I was there. *I hope that you've been having him work on* **his ass kissing** *since then…"*

Kate couldn't help but laugh as she nodded giddily, knowing that it had been just two nights ago when she had him last kneeling behind her paying tribute to her in one of the more humiliating ways that she'd discovered recently. She lost herself in the moment as she pictured her husband's tongue eagerly suckling at her asshole, nude save for his chastity belt as his hands remained fixed on her leather boots at her ankles, when suddenly the break room door swung open and two of their other colleagues walked in, talking loudly and clearly already in a deep conversation of their own.

The budding dominant didn't have to think about her co-worker's plea long while she rinsed her container in the sink nearby before stowing it back in her locker and preparing to return to the floor for the second half of her shift. On her way out the door, she leaned in to Veronica still sitting at the table and demurely inquired, *"So our place Saturday night then???"*

Veronica smiled as she replied, "I think I can move a few things around on my calendar to make that work!"

* * * * * * * * *

Andrew had just walked in the front door with two bags of groceries fresh from the market for the three's dinner when he found his wife frustratingly pacing her way through the house with a clipboard in hand, muttering to herself as she occasionally stopped to scribble something down before moving on to her next point of interest.

"Is everything alright, honey?" Andrew asked quietly as he set the bags down on the island in their kitchen before going over to see what his wife was upset about.

Kate paused and took a deep breath, then held up the clipboard in his direction as he approached and said, "No – *it's not.* We've got company coming over in a few hours and the house looks *terrible!* The floors are dirty; the entire place looks like it hasn't been dusted *in ages…*"

Her husband stuttered as he glanced over to see the thick layer of dust on one of the shelves nearby, *"I'm sorry … I've just been so busy with everything else lately."*

Kate just stared back at him for a moment and chuckled before replying, "You *know* who's coming over tonight … a woman shouldn't be *embarrassed* when another comes over to her home because *her husband* isn't keeping it sufficiently clean for them!”

Andrew took the clipboard from her hands and started to go through her list as he too looked around the room, then sighed as he comforted her, “I’m *really* sorry, Miss Jones. I need to get the groceries put away and start prepping for dinner, but I’ll see what I can do to take care of at least some of these before Miss Greene arrives…”

Kate calmed and a small smile grew over her lips.

“You do that,” she retorted. “I’m going to be upstairs – please do not disturb me until my guest arrives…” she told him as she turned on her heel and marched out of the family room with her husband still left holding the clipboard full of cleaning critiques that she had been collecting for him.

“Yes, ma’am…”

Andrew’s eyes dropped to the floor, but couldn’t but help follow his wife’s feet as she walked down the hall and eventually turned to go up the stairs towards their bedroom. He took a deep breath and gazed over the expansive list that he knew would take *days* to complete, then returned to the kitchen to finish putting things away once he heard their bedroom door close above him.

After taking the time to prepare what he could for the meal he was planning for them all that evening, Andrew then took a second look back over his wife's list and singled out the items that he figured were the most significant and that he could complete in the shortest amounts of time over the next hour and a half that he had to work with before Veronica was set to arrive. Though he felt a little overwhelmed with all of the additional work that was being required of him lately, he didn't dare question it as he hastily dusted and cleaned up various piles of clutter until quickly the time had already passed and he heard the ringing of the doorbell up front…

Feather duster still in hand, Andrew opened the front door to find the perky blonde waiting outside, decked out in a tight, blue dress that showed more leg than it concealed and a matching pair of patent leather pumps that immediately drew his attention. Smiling smugly at him as she took note of what was in his hand, Veronica snickered, "Long time, no see…" as she smirked walking past him into the house as if she owned the place.

"I'll … go let Kate know that you're here…" he stammered

as he watched the sexy twenty-something walk through the room that he had briefly dusted not thirty minutes prior, feeling his cock swell against the sides of its cage before rushing up the stairs to alert his wife of the girl's arrival.

Also taking pleasant note of the duster that her husband carried, Kate randomly glanced around the front room to take note of Andrew's results before walking into the family room where Veronica had made herself comfortable, her designer purse and the large shopping bag that she had brought with her sitting on the ottoman in front of her.

As the two women chatted while Andrew returned to the kitchen to begin cooking dinner, he could hear the occasional giggling but no actual detail as to the discussions that were taking place. Nonetheless he did his best to prepare a meal that he thought his wife would be proud of – this time a braised chicken with mushrooms and almonds, featuring fresh vegetables and one of his wife's all-time favorite red wines. While everything simmered he also set the table for three in the dining room and occasionally slipped back into the front room to continue with his list each time he had a few minutes to spare in the kitchen…

Back in the family room, Veronica was complimenting her

new friend on the transformation that her husband had been through since she'd last been there herself, joking as she pointed out the place on the floor where he had unceremoniously *paid tribute to her fine ass* and then reveling in some of Kate's own stories as she shared some of her own favorites since that fateful night that changed her relationship forever.

At one point in the conversation, Kate stopped abruptly and walked over to pick up a surprisingly large dust bunny that was peeking out from beneath the credenza, muttering in frustration as she grabbed the ball of dust and hair with a tissue and deposited it into a waste basket just around the corner.

"It's just **so hard** *to find good help these days…"* she half joked as she sat back down across from Veronica, prompting a bit of laughter from her guest.

"Ooooh – that actually reminds me … *I brought you something!"* she lit up as she looked over at the shopping bag. "Would your hubby be at a point where I can *borrow him* for a few minutes???"

Kate curiously pondered said gift as she got up and

announced, "Let's find out!" before leading Veronica into the kitchen where they found Andrew taking a pot off of one of the burners while the timer on the oven slowly counted down from 28 minutes.

"How's it coming in here?!" Kate called out playfully as the two entered, with Veronica adding, *"It sure does smell good…"* in a tone that sounded vaguely suspicious as he looked up to see the two attractive women leering over him.

"Good," he replied as he felt himself awkwardly start to swell in his cage again simply on account of their presence. "We're just waiting for the chicken to finish at this point, which should be in another … *37 minutes…"* he reported, glancing up at the timer as he covered the pot in his hand and then turned his attention back to the ladies.

"Excellent!" Veronica exclaimed with an exciting grin as she looked back at her hostess. "So you've got a bit of time to kill … Kate here is going to *hold down the fort* while I show you something in the other room that I brought for her…"

Andrew's heart began to race as his mind immediately went to *the last thing* that Veronica had brought over **that** he had been wearing locked mercilessly around his penis ever since…

Kate just shrugged innocently, though not without a grin herself as her husband looked back to her for any reassurance as to what was about to happen, instead simply saying, *"It'll be just as much of a surprise for me as it is for you!"*

Andrew gulped as he turned to glance into the oven to check on the main course one last time before following Veronica back into the other room to retrieve the large shopping bag that evidently contained the mystery present that she had brought for his wife. Veronica quickly handed the bag off to him to carry, citing, "Let's go upstairs – *I don't want Kate to* **sneak a peek** *until we're ready…"* as she then led him down the hall where he was temporarily pulled aside by his wife who, with Veronica looking on only a few feet away, nonchalantly placed her hand firmly on the steel beneath his belt and whispered into his ear, *"Now whatever is in that bag, I'll expect you to* **do exactly as she says** *and show her the same level of* **obedience** *that you've been showing me these last couple of months …* **are we clear?"**

Andrew stared into his wife's deep, demanding eyes as her grasp continued, eventually whimpering in return,

"…yes, Miss Jones…" after which she released him with a satisfyingly sinister grin, saying to herself, *"Good boy!"* as he retreated up the stairs behind the blonde, carrying her bag in tow just as he'd been directed.

As they stepped around the corner into the master bedroom, Veronica wasted little time shutting the door behind them and then emptying the contents of the shopping bag out onto the bed in front of them. Andrew stood confused at first as he watched her produce what appeared to be a French maid's uniform, but made out of a shiny, vinyl material, followed thereafter by a pair of black pantyhose and then a bright pink shoe box which she opened to reveal a pair of shiny black high heels to match, and finally a long, brown wig with a frilly, maid's cap already pinned into the top of it.

Andrew studied the outfit on the bed for a moment until he finally got up the nerve to ask, "So … *is this another thing that* **he** *wants* **her** *to dress up in???"*

Veronica just snickered back as she fidgeted with the frilly lace that surrounded the edge of the vinyl dress, then laughed, "No – not that I know of, anyways … this is actually *for you!"*

"You see, Kate told me about all of this new housework that you've been taking on lately … *although I see that there are certain areas that sure could use some improvement!* Anyways, I figured that as long as you're *living the part,* you might as well be **dressing the part,** *too."*

Andrew was speechless as his eyes remained locked on the vinyl dress spread out on the bed. The thought of wearing women's clothes had never even crossed his mind before and he couldn't even imagine doing it in front of another person – be it his wife *or* anybody else…

"You want *me* to wear that???" he asked weakly as he felt himself sinking with every moment the shiny vinyl stared back at him from his marital bed.

"Yes!" Veronica replied with a domineering smile. *"Right now."*

He stood in shock while the girl dug through the shopping bag a few moments longer, finally snapping back to reality at the sound of Veronica's fingers as they clicked together before she prompted, "Come on! Dinner's going to be ready soon, isn't it? I'm pretty sure *you* need to be down there to take the chicken out of the oven when that timer goes off, don't you?!"

"What did your wife tell you before you came up here?"

"Alright," Andrew admitted defeat. "What do you want me to do?"

"No – **stop,"** the blonde said emphatically as she glared back at him, standing eye to eye with him in her 5" heels. **"What did your wife tell you??? I want to hear the words come out of your mouth."**

Andrew blushed as his eyes dropped to the floor, quite intimidated as he felt the girl's temper flare. His mind flush with all that was taking place around him, he had to close his eyes for a moment to think back to only five minutes earlier to hear his wife's words whisper once again through his head…

"I'm to do exactly as you say," he stammered, his eyes still locked on the floor, *"and I'm to show you the same level of obedience that I've been showing her…"*

Veronica smirked as she looked down her nose at the submissive man, then ordered, "Take off your clothes, then get down on your knees."

Andrew could practically hear his heart beating out of his chest as he quickly unbuttoned his shirt and threw it on the bed, then did the same with his pants and boxers, leaving only the shiny, steel chastity device that Veronica had locked on him nearly three months earlier. He was barely on his knees for two seconds before he heard her jeer, *"Is* **that** *where those go?!"* pointing back at his clothes, prompting him to get back up and move them to the hamper in the closet before returning to his knees before her once more.

"Put your head on the floor, hands behind your back!" the girl sharply ordered.

The man did as he was told, and seconds later he was starring at those same blue, patent leather pumps only an inch from his face. Raising one foot up to rest on the back of his head, the blonde towered over him as she applied pressure with one foot, causing his brow to rest on the toe of the other.

"This is what you are to women like us – to me, *to your wife,"* Veronica told him bluntly as the sharp heel of her shoe dug into the back of Andrew's head. "You're here for *our entertainment,* and *to serve us*, and that's that."

"Tell me, slave – *are you aroused right now???*"

His haze made him glaze right over what she had called him – it was all he could do to squeak out, *"…yes, Miss Greene…"*

"You know, there's all sorts of stuff that I can teach your wife about this new *lifestyle* that she's growing accustomed to…"

"…and if you think *prancing around in the privacy of your own house in a little maid's outfit* is as bad as it gets, **you have no idea!**"

"Do I need to go downstairs and get the key to *those spikes* that are in your belt, Andrew?" she taunted as she continued to tower dauntingly over him. "I think it's fair to say that Kate would expect me to engage them *all of the way* after what she told you earlier, don't you think?"

"Have you **had them** *engaged* **all of the way,** *yet, Andrew???"*

"No, I haven't, Miss Greene…" he murmured from beneath her feet.

Veronica laughed, remarking, "Well I'll bet that they'd *really* hurt, making mincemeat out of your tiny, little dick … but then again, it's not like it's good for anything else anyways, *now is it, Andrew???"*

"No, Miss Greene – it's not…" he winced as his position balled up on his knees began to get the best of him.

After rocking her heel back and forth and admiring the view a moment longer, Veronica finally posed to the man beneath her, *"So, Andrew – are you going to be* **a good, little hubby** *and put on your uniform like you're told so that you can go finish making us dinner?"*

Without hesitation, the man replied back simply, *"Yes, Miss Greene…"*

"You know," Veronica laughed as she took her heel off of the man's head and stepped back away from where he was kneeling, "I think we're probably done with *the formalities* between us. You should really be calling me **Mistress,** and the next time you're in front of your wife like this, I want you to call *her* that, too."

"Yes … *Mistress,"* Andrew said quietly as he sat up from his position, though still clasping his wrists behind his back.

Before he was told to get up, the blonde then paced back and forth in front of her subject a few times finally stopping and this time more playfully asking, *"Do you like* **my shoes,** *Andrew?"*

"Kate tells me that you've been really into *keeping her shoes neat and organized* for her, so what do you think of mine? Would you like to *kiss them* as a symbol of how we've grown here just now?"

Andrew looked up at the woman standing over him in her short, blue dress and the heels that he had just finished being given an up close introduction to, and a moment later the words fell from his mouth as if they had been the most natural part of his vocabulary all of his life…

"Yes, Mistress…"

Veronica chuckled to herself.

"Then stick out your tongue, slave…"

As the man knelt there at the foot of his marital bed, naked except for the steel belt locked around his genitals, he took another deep breath and then obediently extended his tongue while the blonde slipped off her shoes, then took one of the shiny, blue pumps in her hand and brought to rest just the very toe of its underside on the end of Andrew's awaiting, wet tongue. The girl held her shoe there triumphantly for a few seconds while he glanced from her and then back again to the shoe in front of him, confused but not daring to question her until she finally laughed again and tipped the heel forward, forcing his nose into the pocket of the shoe defiantly before pulling back and slipping them both back on her feet.

"Did you like that **smell?!"** she jeered as she laughed down at him once more. *"You're not worthy to kiss my shoes … at least* **not yet,** *anyways…"*

"Now get up and put your dress on!" Veronica continued, her voice a playful tone in her head, though at that point it was being interpreted as anything but by her plaything.

Clueless on where to begin, Andrew looked down at the pile of female clothes spread out on the bed and first picked up the uniform itself, though Veronica was quick to correct him by suggesting that the pantyhose go on first. Sliding the smooth, restricting nylon carefully up one leg, then the other, he couldn't help but notice the cool sensations that rose up his body, stopping just above his thighs where he lifted the waistband over his chastity belt like a perfect fit.

He then stood obediently as Veronica took the vinyl maid's outfit and unzipped the back before holding it out in front of him, allowing him to briefly use her arm for support as he lifted his second leg into the sleeve, unsure of what to think as he then felt the girl slide the dress up his torso until it came time to slip his arms into each of the short sleeves at his shoulders. When dress was fitted in place, she then slowly guided the small zipper up the man's back until it came to rest between his shoulder blades.

Before he had a chance to even look down at himself and whatever it was that the girl was creating, Veronica had disappeared back to the shopping bag for a brief moment to produce what looked like a pair of silicon breast implants, as he soon noticed that *the bust* of the uniform was presently a bit *empty* for someone of his stature without proper breasts of his own. The breast forms quickly changed all of that, however, and once Veronica had slipped each of the two jiggly sacks into the cups of the dress, it seemed to fill out quite nicely and was very evidently to the Mistress's satisfaction…

"Have you ever walked in high heels before?" she asked

him with a straight face, though Andrew just looked back at her with a blank look, far from the type who would ever dare to do such a thing even just for something like Halloween once a year.

She directed him to sit down on the edge of the bed, and while Andrew began to taking curious note of the smooth vinyl that was hugging his midsection, Veronica had grabbed the black heels from the shoe box next to him and one shoe at a time fitted the high heels to the man's pantyhose-laden feet, securing each with the cute, buckling ankle strap that had attracted her to them before moving on to the other.

"Ok, now just stand up nice and slow…" Veronica directed him after buckling the second shoe into place. Andrew was so far outside of anything he'd ever known, it was all that he could do to simply put both of his feet on the floor, taking note of the awkward, new position that the shoes held his feet in, and then carefully did his best to stand up on the 5" spikes, reaching out to his interrogator once again for stability as he tried to find his balance on the shoes that he'd always found *beyond sexy* when worn by anyone of the opposite sex…

"Good," she replied curtly as she took his hand from her shoulder and then let it drop. "Now walk to the closet and back – *small steps…*"

Andrew did just that, moving only a few inches at a time as he teetered on the ridiculously high heels while Veronica first watched for a few minutes and then retreated back to her shopping bag to root around in it some more while he practiced walking in small circles around the room and then just standing in one place on the perilous heels. He didn't even know how to acknowledge it at the time, but the more he walked, he began to notice the pleasant swaying of the heavy, vinyl skirt as it fell mid-thigh with each step, and although he felt more exposed and vulnerable than ever before, his curiosity couldn't help but take him over to his wife's full length mirror to consider his new uniform in its entirety.

He looked **ridiculous,** he knew … yet taking his own body out of the equation, the vinyl maid's uniform by itself did look *incredibly sexy,* coupled with the stilettos on his feet and even the sheer, dark pantyhose that bridged the two. There was something about the frilly, white apron that had been attached around the waist of the dress, and the corresponding lace that was found at every edge from the neckline to the sleeves and even around the bottom edge … the entire outfit was *undeniably feminine* and he would've killed to see his wife or anyone else in it.

…anyone else but him…

"Ok, so let's get you finished up," the blonde's voice snapped him back into the present once more. *"I'm hungry!"*

In her hands as she approached from the side was something that it didn't recognize – it appeared to be a piece of rubber that was flesh-toned, in the shape of the lower half of a person's face. He guessed that the person was intended to be a woman on account of the shiny shade of pink that the lips had been painted…

"What's that?" he asked before he even realized that the question was out of character.

Veronica quickly shot back, *"This* is to prevent you from *asking too many questions* **like that!** *Remember, a maid's role is* **to listen** *and* **to serve,** *not to speak…"*

When she flipped over the rubber in her hands, it was only then that he pieced together that it was some sort of bondage gag – on account of the straps that hung from either side as well as the rubber insert on the inside that seemed to be located just opposite those pink, shiny lips. Andrew wasn't given the opportunity to ask any more questions at that point as the blonde made light work of offering the mask up to his face and then inserting the rubber bulb into his mouth.

Andrew had never worn any type of gag before, but as Veronica began to cinch the straps behind his head that served to meld his face and the mask as one, he felt the bulb too being pulled tighter between his lips until he was pretty sure that any words he attempted to speak would just come out as a muffled mess to those around him. The look on his face was a bizarre one, as the rubber mask covered his entire mouth up to below his nose, then wrapping all the way around his jaw line to the back of his head. The centerpiece of the mask, of course, were those shiny, pink lips that now took the place of his own, beaming a permanent smile with dimples to spare that seemed to go along with the rest of the outfit despite leaving Andrew feeling more awkward than ever.

"Don't worry – we're almost done…" the blonde reassured him with a wink as she finished manipulating the buckles behind his head and then jumped right into fitting the long, brown wig on top, leaving her victim speechless in more ways than one as he watched helplessly the transformation taking place in the mirror in front of him. Veronica expertly used a number of pins to hold the hair down to his head, testing it with her own hands in several directions before she was satisfied, then ducking into the attached bathroom to grab one of Kate's brushes to better arrange the outcome…

"Almost there!" she told the dumbstruck man once she set down the brush and traded it a moment later for a pair of large, hoop earrings that were in the bottom of the bag which she proceeded to clip onto the dangling lobes of each of Andrew's ears without missing a beat before disappearing once again – this time to her hostess's vanity – in search of a few final touches that she felt *her masterpiece* was missing.

"Now just hold still and this will all be over soon," Veronica offered her mute subject as she produced a handful of tubes from Kate's makeup with the intent of making the maid's eyes match the fake smile that was now plastered across her face. Andrew simply stood there in defeat as the cute blonde expertly attacked the remaining portion of his face with a myriad of brushes and pens until looking back at himself in the mirror, it was still clear as day that he was *a man in women's clothes* … but his eyes *did* seem to sparkle a bit more than they had in the past…

"DONE!" she finally announced triumphantly as she put the hair brush and makeup back where she had found them before returning to Andrew's side, quite amused at the result in the mirror as her subject still looked back in shock and as submissive as ever. Putting an arm around him and then casually running her other hand over the smooth, black vinyl of the dress, and even gently tapping at his crotch in its steel sheath that was barely concealed under the skimpy skirt, Veronica eventually landed her other hand on the maid's waist as she leaned in and quietly purred, *"So tell me, Andrew – are you aroused* **now???"**

The look on the man's face was one of confusion and fear as he stared back at himself alongside the beautiful woman, the bizarre comparison that he was himself on his own pair of shiny, black heels. He tried to speak, but the gag wedged in his mouth made little work of the words that he strived to produce, and instead he was reduced merely to body language as he quietly and ever-so-subtly nodded his head in a truly debilitated response.

A sadistic smile grown on the girl's face as a result, Veronica quietly whispered, *"I wish that I had the key to those chastity spikes on me right now so that I could turn them up* **just because..."** as she reached around and groped the man in his uniform as he continued to just stand there paralyzed.

After a few moments of leering over her latest kinky creation, Veronica finally looked Andrew in his strikingly made up eyes as she put his masked chin in her hands and seductively told him, *"Now let's get you back in that kitchen where you belong..."*

* * * * * * * * * *

"Are you ready?!" Veronica called down the stairs as she led the way with her newest creation only a few steps behind.

"Can't wait!" Kate called back as she randomly stirred one of the pots on the stove to keep herself busy while she passed the time. Walking back to where the entrance to the kitchen met the hallway, she waited with curious anticipation to see what the feisty blonde had cooked up for her this time as she heard the two slowly walking back down the stairs, with Veronica's bubbly face the first to pop out into the hallway, then followed a moment later by a sight that Kate *definitely* would've never expected…

"Oh my god!!!" Kate laughed uncontrollably, clasping her hands over her mouth as her husband appeared *in his new uniform*, wobbling down the stairs on the tedious 5" stilettos as the shiny, vinyl skirt flowed around his thighs, his head covered by the long, brown hair of the wig that Veronica had pinned to his head not ten minutes earlier.

"Well what do we have here?!" his wife exclaimed in great amusement as she stepped around to take a good look at her husband in drag, his head sheepishly dropping as he stood helpless and humiliated in front of her. She first lifted up the edge of the dress, grinning widely as she confirmed that his chastity belt still stood firmly in place, then let the vinyl drop as she slipped her hand down his pantyhose-clad thigh and moved her eyes slowly up his body seductively until eventually reaching his face to find a number of new surprises…

Kate audibly smirked as she looked into her husband's eyes and saw the quick application of dark greys and bright pink that made up the maid's eye shadow, then reached a hand up to pull back his brown hair to reveal the clip-on hoop earrings that he wore … though clearly what fascinated her the most was the rubber appendage that covered the lower part of her husband's face including his mouth.

Running her thumb gently over the supple, pink lips that had been sculpted into the mask as she cradled her man's chin, Kate's laughter continued as she glanced over at Veronica and asked her with a giggle, *"He's **gagged** under here, isn't he?!"*

Veronica smiled as she raised her eyebrows suggestively, asking, "You like what you see?!"

Without missing a beat, Kate shot back a moment later, "I like what I'm *not hearing!"* rolling her eyes at her husband as she continued to chuckle at his predicament as she finished her circle around him, thoroughly amusing herself all the more as she took notice of the blushed look on what she could see of her husbands face as the two women delighted in his torment.

*"*At first he wanted to know if the outfit was something *that your doctor friend wanted to see* **you** *dressed up in!"* the blonde snickered as she admired the woman preying on her own husband.

"Hmmmmmm…" Kate thought out loud as she studied the uniform further with a mischievous look in her eye. "I can see Marcus being down for a little *role playing!*"

"And I **love** *the shoes!"* she added. *"Those are good* **fucking heels** *right there…"*

"Think she'll be able to stay balanced on them tonight while she's *serving our meal?"* Veronica then posed as she began to walk down the hall towards the kitchen.

"Well I hope she's a fast learner *because she doesn't really have much of a choice!"* Kate chimed in response as she too began walking, leaving her new maid a few steps behind as Andrew focused on short steps - *beat red as far as he could tell* - as he followed the two women back into the kitchen, listening intently as they chuckled at his expense the whole way.

"Don't just stand there – *you've got a meal to finish!"* Kate jeered playfully as she watched her husband pause as his heels met the tile for the first time.

She then turned back to her guest and asked, "So, did you do her nails, too??? That would make this evening a new challenge for her…"

Veronica grinned at her friend's quick adoption of the female pronoun to identify her husband, replying, "No, we didn't really have time … *a nice French tip would've gone really well* … and I wouldn't have minded having her *shave her legs, too.*"

"Really, just about *all of her nasty body hair!*" Kate added in with a laugh.

"But I *was* happy with what little I did with *her makeup* in such short order," Veronica said. "I think I was able to do a pretty good job matching her makeup to the mask with what I had to work with…"

*"And I **love** that mask already!!!"* Kate gushed as she looked back over to see her husband turning his direction back to the oven where it was required. *"No **complaining,** no* **protests…"**

"*…just what the dominant woman ordered!*" Veronica finished the thought with a devilish grin.

"Of course, what I *wanted to do* but wasn't able to for you…" she then added with a sly grin, "was *engage some of those* **chastity spikes** *to keep our new maid here* **on pointe** *throughout the evening…"*

Kate beamed a huge grin as she walked over to where her purse was sitting and happily reported, *"Well, we can go ahead and do that* **right now!"** as she produced the keys both to his chastity belt *and* to the spikes from the bottom of her black leather handbag.

Andrew's heart raced as he heard her walk up behind him, knowing already what was next in store as he set down the wooden spoon in his hand and turned to face her, his eyes on the ground though he towered considerably over her in the tall heels…

"Legs spread, hands behind your back," she told him with a persistent grin as she knelt down before him, then added, *"…and* **hold your dress!"** as she waited for him to lift it away to reveal the heavy, steel belt that he'd endured for the past three months in her new service. Making quick work to fit the tiny wrench into the slot at the base of the tube, Andrew winced as he heard her count out loud, *"One …* *two…"* while the tiny, pin-like pricks were driven into his mysteriously swollen member until Kate finally stood up and told him, *"There are* **two of us,** *so two clicks work … for*

now…"

Kate then locked eyes with her husband underneath the mask as he let his dress float back around his legs, and lowered her voice as she stared back at him, *"Do they hurt???"*

All he could do was slowly nod as he felt himself trapped in the dominant woman's gaze.

"Good," she purred as she seductively stared back at him. *"Well you'd better* **serve us well** *here tonight in your new role or you might spend* **the rest of the weekend** *in your new, little* **sissy uniform***, strung up in my closet with your wrists handcuffed behind your back as you learn* **just how painful** *shoes like that can be when a girl is forced to stand on them* **all night long…"**

He watched her hazel eyes seem to flare with intensity as she snickered in his face before finally turning to throw the keys back into her purse, muttering, *"Now get back to work,* **slut!"** as she took Veronica back into the family room where the two continued reeling in their amusement of all that was transpiring, to the tune of clanging silverware *and* the click of Andrew's high heels as he clomped clumsily between the kitchen and dining room, trying his best to finish up the final touches in preparation for their meal.

Their chatter continued like never before over the next twenty minutes as Veronica enlightened Kate to even more ways to *transform* her husband, with at one point the two coming to the unanimous decision that Andrew's *maid name* without a doubt had to be **"Andrea"** until the subject of their amusement finally appeared in the doorway, unable to say a word and instead having to *point* back in the direction of the dining room to indicate that dinner was almost ready.

With her husband still in earshot, it was then that the blonde leaned in close and whispered one last surprise into Kate's ear that left her wide-eyed, bearing an ear-to-ear grin on her face as she suddenly and quite enthusiastically excused herself to go get changed before dinner…

While he waited for his wife to return, Andrew began to carry each of the impeccable dishes that he had created out to the table set for three, with the homemade biscuits and fresh vegetables first, followed by a full wine glass for each place setting, and finally the main course to sit in the center of the table, proudly as in his opinion one of his best dishes to date … though he hadn't been able to *taste test* his creation on this particular evening.

Andrew was just about ready to sit down and wait for his wife's arrival when he *very unexpectedly* heard a knock at the door. Within a second, a petrified look took over his face when he realized the ramifications of his current attire. Panicking, he first looked over to Veronica who was seated nearby, yet she simply scoffed back at him, "What are you looking at me for – don't you think it's *the maid's responsibility* to answer the door?!"

He protested into the gag, but only a muffled whine was heard throughout the kitchen as the blonde glanced back over at him and first smirked, then changed to all out laughter as she told him, "If you think those spikes hurt now, just think how they're going to feel if you make her come down to get that herself before she's ready…"

Fear dominated over him as he considered her comment while he slowly walked through the house towards the front door. When he finally reached the door, Andrew paused just long enough for the knock to rap against the wood separating them for the third time, triggering his wife to call out, *"Are you going to get that or what?!"*

Biting his lip underneath the mask as he sighed, Andrew then reached out and turned the knob, slowly opening the door to reveal a face that he'd seen once before…

"I *am* at the right place, aren't I?" the tall, black man asked with a small smile under his lips before adding, *"I didn't know that* **Kate had gotten herself a maid…"**

Andrew stood in shock as he stared back at Dr. Marcus Powers, the man who had been *fucking his wife* and who had ultimately encouraged her to take their lifestyle down the crazy road that he'd been enduring for the past three months. He didn't know what to say, though the gag strapped around his lips would've prevented any commentary that he had to say to the man, anyways, and before he was able to offer up any reaction other than pure shock, Andrew heard his wife's won excitement from behind him as she rushed to greet their unexpected guest.

"She just told me that you were coming!" he heard Kate gush from across the room, stepping back with the doorknob still in hand as he watched her fall into the doctor's arms like they'd been separated for years. Marcus kept no secrets making his affections for the married woman known, pulling his arms around her waist and lifting Kate into him as the two shared a passionate kiss only a foot from Andrew's face as he smelled the sweet scent of his wife's

perfume wafting off of her body while she pulled herself closer with both arms wrapped around the man's neck.

As the two embraced nearly on top of him with Andrew left awkwardly holding the door open, he couldn't help but focus in on his wife's change of dress for the embarrassing night's turn of events. Whereas before when Veronica had arrived, Kate had been dressed fairly low key in a simple sundress, she had recently changed into something much more provocative – his eyes first took in the sexy, black leather skirt that fell several inches above her knees and had been paired with an equally pair of leather knee-high riding boots, all topped with a shiny, red satin halter top that showed off both her arms and her chest rather alluringly … both of which currently had the doctor's attention as he watched nervously as their nearly pornographic kiss continued while he dug his hands in and openly groped her through the tight, leather skirt…

When their lips finally separated, the two lingered a moment longer while Kate giddily flirted with her latest guest, purring, *"It's so good to see you…"* as she stole a few more pecks before sinking back down onto her heels. She then took him by the hand and led him into the house, saying not a word to her husband save for shouting over her shoulder, *"Andrea, do close the door before we get a draft in here…"* on their way into the dining room.

As Andrew himself reached the kitchen, he stared at the cabinets blankly for a few minutes, unsure of what to make of his wife's latest unexpected exhibit of flaunting her adulterous lifestyle while his heart seemed like it would beat clear out of his chest, until finally he took a deep breath and decided to make the best of it, retrieving a fourth set of table sittings from the cabinet and preparing to join them out in the dining room when instead Kate appeared at the doorway, wagging her finger once she realized his intention with the extra plate in his hands…

"What do you think you're doing???" she asked him with the same sharp tone in her voice from earlier, though her cheeks were still red from laughing so hard at his expense earlier. *"The help doesn't eat at the dining room table … you'll eat whatever leftovers are available after the rest of us are done."*

Kate gloated on her husband's appearance a moment longer as he nervously put the plate down on the counter, then slowly started to snicker as she looked him over once more before catching his eyes once again and laughing, *"You look so …* **ridiculous** *… this is* **perfect!"**

Still giggling as she turned to rejoin her guests, Kate stopped just before the doorway and confessed, "That's right – I almost forgot!" and walked back over to her purse, retrieving the same wrench to adjust the spikes inside of his chastity belt as before.

"*…three … oh, what the hell …* **four!"** she cackled as she turned the spikes up higher than they had ever been before.

"Just because…" she whispered into her sissified husband's ear before snickering once again to herself, then tossing the wrench into her purse nearby, this time zipping it shut and preparing to take it with her back into the dining room when instead she paused with a smirk on her face, got up in his face once more and told him sharply, *"If you want to* **worship my ass,** *you've got 30 seconds…"*

Kate then turned away from her maid of a husband and waited, shaking her leather-skirted ass playfully as she laughed out loud until he finally gave in and got down on his knees behind her. Staring directly at the sleek, black leather that was stretched beautifully over his wife's bottom, Andrew was overwhelmed with a mix of emotions as he reached down and took Kate's booted ankles in each of his hands just like before, though this time instead of being presented with his wife's humiliating, yet bizarrely enchanting asshole to degrade himself on with his very tongue, between him and her ass was both the tight leather of the skirt *and* the rubber mask that had been strapped around his mouth all evening.

Although he did his best to press his face against the fine leather just the same, Kate couldn't help but laugh as she savored his predicament, taunting him, *"Oh well — it looks like* **even my ass** *is off limits to you tonight!"*

Then while he remained focused on the leather, she discretely reached over to her purse and retrieved her phone, which she was able to use to snap a perfect selfie from above of her dressed to the nines and *her husband kneeling behind her as pitiful as ever…*

Kate then leaned her ass back into his face as she teased him further, "Remember where *his hands were?!* All for him and none for my little sissy-locked husband, *and I'll bet there's a lot yet to come before this night is over…"*

Looking over her shoulder and taking in every element of the moment at hand, Kate found herself on cloud nine as she felt the surge of sexuality in lowering her husband further than she ever had before. It was a new high like no other, and as she snapped a couple more shots of the former man dressed in his high heels and vinyl dress, kneeling at her feet, she then strode back in the dining room with her purse in hand as if she was on top of the world, even stopping off at her lover's spot at the table to find a seat on his lap and steal another sensual kiss while it was all Veronica could do to look on in wild amusement, she herself also laughing at the predicament that the two had placed the cross-dressed maid kneeling on the floor back in the kitchen into with a great sense of accomplishment.

Andrew knelt on the floor until his knees hurt more than the spikes driving into his chastised penis as the scent of his wife's leather skirt fucked with his mind supreme, truly baffled as to what all was taking place and even more significantly, *why he continued to throb and swell with a distinct arousal beneath his belt even after all that his wife and her friends were putting him through…*

He finally got himself together enough to stand up and put back away the dishware that he'd gotten out for himself, then fell back into his role by doing his best to clean up what he had prepared that afternoon in the kitchen until he finally heard his wife calling him by name to come in.

...or at least by **the new feminine name** *that he had somehow become...*

"Oh, Andrea ... you can come and clear the table now, dear..." Kate sang with a newfound cheer in her voice, smiling smugly as her new maid appeared in the doorway a moment later, *silent but to serve* as Andrew walked around the table gathering plates and silverware without making eye contact with any one of them. After making several trips back and forth with piles of empty dishes in hand, all that was left was their glasses and the bottle of wine, which Andrew picked up from its stand and offered outward to his wife with a simple gesture.

"Excellent!" she smiled as she pushed her nearly empty wine glass in his direction to be topped off, grinning proudly as he then proceeded to do the same for the others – first Veronica, then even the doctor to her other side – before disappearing back into the kitchen to dispose of the empty bottle.

As he returned and then sheepishly realized that there was nothing else for him to do as he wobbled in his heels, it was then that Marcus spoke up, *"Those are quite the pair of stilettos your maid is wearing in service tonight, my dear!"*

He froze, his eyes darting over to his wife as she cheerfully replied, "Yes, but she's got to learn sometime! Besides, Andrea here seems to have quite the thing for high heels – *as you might remember* … so I say it's about time she learn to *suffer in them* like the rest of us…"

"Oh, *but you suffer in them* **so beautifully,** *my sweet,*" the doctor flirted back with her, his eyes only casually glancing back to Andrew, though still not looking him in the eye. "I could see you wearing a pair of *slut heels* like those yourself!"

"Only if you buy them for me!" she giggled back as she reached over and placed a hand on the man's thigh.

As Marcus painfully stood there in his vinyl uniform, his eyes unsure of where to look as they begged to wander over in his wife's direction despite knowing quite distinctly what they would find there, Marcus took things a step further and drove the humiliation home with his next line…

"Well if your new maid is so fond of footwear, maybe she wouldn't have a problem **polishing mine while I'm fucking you once we're done with dinner here in a bit…"**

Kate took the lead hook, line, and sinker as she replied

merrily, *"Well I'm done* **now** *if you are!"*

Veronica couldn't help but burst out laughing as she took the opportunity to get up from the table, though she didn't make it out of the room towards the bathroom before Kate retained her attention by snapping her fingers and pointing down to the floor between her and her lover, gesturing for Andrew to *remove the man's shoes from his feet himself* before the two would slip away to savor each other's carnal impulses while he was left in the most humiliating of situations.

Down on the floor, Andrew could barely see straight as he inched closer to the pair's shoes, noticing how flirtatiously close to one another they had been throughout dinner as he first stared at his wife's leather boots and imagined being ungagged and thus able to service them properly. But instead he was forced to look over at the doctor's shoes — a very expensive-looking pair of brown loafers, which he reached out to untie with a lump in his throat, whimpering to himself as the odor of the man's feet overwhelmed any more desirable scents that he'd picked up from his wife's delectable ensemble.

"Now you be careful with those — they cost more than you make in a week!" Marcus jeered playfully as the maid resurfaced, taking an extra moment to figure out how to stand back up on his heels from the floor, then taking the doctor's shoes in his hands and standing patiently next to the dining room table while he waited for his wife's interjection…

Instead Veronica spoke up as the two were beginning to rise from the table, saying, "Well *I'm* going to get going and give *the two of you* a little privacy!" thereafter adding with a wink to Kate, "But I may stick around for just a short while to *help your new maid get started on the rest of the chores that you laid out for her earlier…*"

"Of course!" Kate replied with a grin as she took a step over and put an arm around Marcus as if the two were a couple. "I'm sure she can use all of the help that she can get – *she doesn't want to start off* **owing my dear Marcus right off the bat** *by somehow ruining his shoes…*"

"I believe you'll find a jar of shoe polish under the sink."

With that Andrew stood watching the two as they walked in each other's arms into the family room, his last look at his wife as beautiful as he'd ever seen her as she turned to glide closed the sliding French doors that formally separated the two rooms.

The look on her face was devastatingly domineering as she enjoyed every fiber of his submission, about to culminate in the sweetest way imaginable at the time as she raised her eyebrows seductively at him before disappearing behind the door, leaving Andrew left standing there head to toe in drag and holding her lover's shoes while the young blonde who had helped to orchestrate it all looked on with a mischievous grin of her own.

* * * * * * * * *

"Baby, I've never felt like this before…" Kate told her lover as the two slipped onto the white leather couch whose back fell to the wall that was shared with the dining room. *"… tonight was* **perfect** *– I don't think I* **ever** *want to go back to the way it was before!"*

Marcus smiled as he pulled the woman on top of him and slid the soft, leather skirt up her thighs.

"So you had no idea what Veronica had planned to do tonight?!" the doctor asked suspiciously as he caressed her breasts through the shimmery top.

"Nope – did you?!"

He grinned as he admitted, "I knew she was up to *something,* but I had no idea she'd ever take it *that* far!"

"…but *you* seem to be enjoying it quite a bit!" he added as he cradled the woman's ass while she arched her back away from him in delight.

"He's so … **powerless!"** she boasted as she began to roll her hips softly against the bulge growing underneath his slacks. *"I feel like I could do* **anything that I want** *to him!!!"*

Kate grinned with pleasure as she felt herself free of any inhibitions, about to break the vows of her marriage *in her own home* while her husband cleaned dishes in the next room, *and yet somehow all of it built up together to just feel* **wonderfully naughty** *instead of in any way* **wrong…**

"The only problem is," she continued as she enjoyed the man's touch while she sat stewing deliciously in his lap, "that I don't really know *what to do with him."*

"I mean, I know that I like him kissing my feet, *or my shoes."*

"And that chastity belt has been *the best thing that you ever bought me!"*

Marcus smiled proudly.

"But like, tonight," she continued, slowly starting to pant a bit as Marcus played with her nipples through her red satin top while she spoke. "I would've never thought of that, *but I was on cloud nine seeing him all dressed up as a* **little sissy bitch** *like that!"*

"You liked seeing him *humiliated,* did you?" he asked her with a sly grin as he reached up underneath her skirt and caught the band of her panties, which he proceeded to remove and toss to the side with little resistance from his host as she simply nodded eagerly in response to his question.

"And you like seeing him *beneath you?"* he continued as he unbuckled his belt and smoothly slid his pants and boxers down to his ankles before returning the married woman quickly to his lap.

"Absolutely!" Kate groaned as she felt his bare cock rubbing up against her pussy.

"Well then there are *all sorts of things* that are at your

disposal now, my dear," he explained to her warmly as he savored her touch against his cock a few humps longer before finally taking her by the waist and guiding her down onto his shaft right there in the middle of her family room.

"There's torture and discipline…" he continued.

"Bondage…"

"Tease and denial … **which I might add you seem to already be turning into quite the expert in!"**

"There are so many things, my pet," he groaned as Kate leaned forward and kissed him deeply while she continued to slowly and sensuously grind against him with all of her pent up excitement now focused solely on him.

"I want to hear them all…" Kate moaned into his lips between kisses.

"Teach me how to make him **my slave…"**

"…my slut…"

Marcus untied the halter behind her neck and began to more openly grope her exposed breasts as he then asked her, *"So if I teach you how to make him* **your slave,** *does that still mean that you're going to be* **mine?!"**

Kate tipped her head back in ecstasy as she started to pick up rhythm bouncing on the thick cock between her legs.

"I'll be anything you want me to be, Sir!" she moaned as he began sucking on one of her nipples while twisting the other between his fingers. Before she was able to cum, he soon stood up with her still in his arms and then flipped her over so that she was now kneeling on the end of the couch with her ass up in the air at just the perfect height.

"Make me **your slave girl…"** Kate moaned as he resumed pounding her with an astounding vigor from his new vantage point.

"Silly bitch – **you already are!"** he laughed back as he slapped her ass hard enough for it to echo throughout the entire house…

* * * * * * * * *

"Somebody's having fun in there…" Veronica snickered as she watched Andrew carefully polishing the first of the man's shoes in the kitchen as they both heard his slap of Kate's

ass plain as day two rooms away.

"But *it's good* that she found somebody who can do *that* to her, you know," the blonde added wholeheartedly. "Every woman deserves to have *that* in her life."

The girl paced blindly around the kitchen while Andrew worked, sipping her glass and generally poking her nose around until some twenty minutes had passed and he was finally setting down the other shoe in completion. She walked over to inspect his work and couldn't deny that the expensive shoes did look considerably shinier than they did when he had first taken them off of their owner's feet. Just as Andrew seemed ready for a break, clearly tired after wearing the tall shoes for the past several hours, she then picked up the clipboard that he had been working from for Kate earlier and beckoned him with a single finger to follow her into the great room out front…

* * * * * * * * *

"That was wonderful … *you're wonderful…*" Kate gushed as she lay collapsed in a heap on one of the couches, wearing only her leather skirt high around her hips and her favorite riding boots, which seemed amusingly appropriate to her given what she'd just done for an after-dinner extracurricular.

Marcus laughed.

"Says the woman who fucks *like a goddess!* You make my job *easy,* and I swear, if it keeps getting better like this *the kinkier you get,* I'm gonna have to get Veronica to teach you *everything that* **she knows** *on top of everything that I know!"*

Kate giggled gleefully along with him as she replied, "Yeah, I *definitely* think that I'm going to have to start hanging out with *her* some more…"

"She's a feisty one, that's for sure!" he laughed

A few minutes later once they had both caught their breath, he inquired, "It's getting kind of late – so do you think my shoes are ready???"

Kate grinned widely as she replied, *"What do I get to do to him if they're not?!"*

"The same thing that you get to do to him **if they are … that's the beauty of being a domme, my dear!"** he offered back.

"Hmmmmm … *Mistress Katherine,*" she purred excitedly. "Kind of has a nice ring to it, don't you think?"

"Just as long as you're still eager to be *Slave Girl Kate* in my arms!" Marcus ribbed back at her as he slid over and scooped the woman into his arms and into his lips.

"But of course, Master!" she cooed as the two kissed sublimely, first tenderly and then a bit deeper as Marcus's hand wandered between Kate's legs and was quite pleased with what he had found.

Sliding her underneath him and then climbing on top of her in one fell swoop as his growing cock found her quite well spent mound once more, he gently pushed himself inside of her and leaned in close, whispering into her ear, *"You know, if you want to get started on that next level with him* **tonight…"**

* * * * * * * * *

An entranced and exhausted Andrew didn't even hear Kate walking her friend back to the front door, though he couldn't help but watch out of the corner of his eye as the two shared one last long and passionate embrace until she finally closed the door behind him while he continued dusting every surface around their great room that had been sorely neglected for far too long. His wife walked on by him once more without saying a word, though she returned a few minutes later to more closely inspect his progress before finally speaking up.

"It's looking better in here, but you've definitely still got a lot of work to do," she critiqued as she admired the shelves that he'd just recently dusted, then ran her finger over a window sill that he clearly hadn't.

He continued dusting in his zone as she commented once again on his kinky attire, joking, "Black vinyl *does* look good on you!" and then adding later from another angle, "But I'll bet those heels are just about *killing you* by now…"

Then taking the duster out of his hand and setting it on one of the shelves, Kate gently but forcefully grabbed the maid by her long, brown wigged hair and guided her down to her knees, putting her eye to eye with the black leather skirt that she had since returned to its usual position before seeing Marcus out, then took her husband's masked chin between her thumb and fingers as she spoke.

"You're probably just about ready to come out of this thing, aren't you? I guess I never really thought about it, but **it's got to be pretty tough to eat dinner with a gagged mouth…"**

Andrew made not a sound, but simply dropped his head, his eyes landing on those same riding boots that even then he confusingly could only think of dropping down to worship on his wife's feet.

"Stay right there," Kate told him as she suddenly walked away, though going only as far as to retrieve her purse from the dining room before returning and producing the same silver handcuffs that she had used on him before. First helping him to stand up again, then handing him the cuffs and telling him to put them on … which he did *behind his back* without question, she then produced the familiar chastity spike wrench from her bag and knelt to disengage them from their most painful state.

Andrew heard three clicks out of four, which didn't remove the spikes entirely but was still a considerable relief compared to the last several hours, although already in his mind alongside the gratitude that he felt loomed the next question of *what price he would have to pay for her mercy.*

"It's been a pretty wild night!" Kate snickered as she moved behind him and closed the handcuffs another notch tighter before using the opposite end of the key to double-lock them both into place.

"And I'm feeling *generous,*" she continued, "so I think I'm going to let you take off that mask … *I'm* **not sure** *about the rest of it yet because* … **it suits you…"**

She laughed openly as she dressed him down even though they were the only two left in the house, thereafter explaining, "There are going to be *two rules* when that gag comes out of your mouth … do you understand me?"

"Rule #1 – *Don't say a word … no talking, no groaning, no moaning unless you're really eager to have those rubber lips buckled back around your face for the rest of the weekend!"*

"Rule #2 – *And this should really apply* **going forward,** *not just to tonight, but you will* **always obey** *whatever Mistress Katherine tells you to* … **without question."**

"You **live to worship me,"** Kate added with a sinister tone to her voice, *"and once I take that gag out of your mouth, you're going to* **drop to your knees** *and* **kiss my boots** *to accept that*

pact … just like I know you've been dreaming of doing all night long…"

Andrew soaked in every last word that fell from his wife's sharp tongue, desperate to do just that and whatever else she had in store for him as he stood before her bound and humiliated, but never more drawn to her. He already felt but an ant in her presence after knowing how blatantly she had enjoyed fucking her lover under their own roof that evening, yet instead of animosity towards this woman who sought to rule his life, he found himself overwhelmed in subservience and was felt desperate yet for another way to show her.

Seeing the fire in her eyes as she turned, Kate gestured for him to follow as she walked back through the house to the hallway, then began to climb up the stairs leading to their master bedroom. She pointed for him to kneel on the floor at the edge of the bed, then after unbuckling the mask and tossing it carelessly off to the side, she climbed up on the bed in front of him, hiked her skirt up, and then also removed her very wet panties and tossed them away as well…

It was then as Kate spread her legs and showed her husband

the used and abused pussy that her lover had left behind after that passionate evening, she explained to him with a gleam in her eye, *"On second thought, you can worship my boots afterwards … but first,* **Marcus left one more thing that I want you to clean up."**

Her
New Cuckold
...Humiliated

Her New Cuckold ...
Humiliated

That's right – **every last drop..."** Kate cackled as she looked down at her husband's face buried between her legs.

Though he was barely recognizable from her perspective, still dressed in the long, brown wig and black vinyl maid's uniform that Veronica had put him in earlier that afternoon, the view was second to none as she savored in her husband's humiliation, watching him lick the very cum from her pussy that her lover Marcus had left behind barely an hour earlier. It had been the first time that she'd fucked him without a condom, and yet as she stared in awe at the incredible exchange of power taking place between her legs at that very moment, she knew that it opened up possibilities that she'd never be able to deny again…

"When did you become such a little bitch?" she taunted as she ran her fingers through the wig on his head and grabbed hard, forcing his face even closer to her pussy as his tongue seemed to eagerly lap the cum that slowly dripped from her folds.

"My little bitch…" Kate continued to muse, glancing over to the wedding photos that hung on the wall and laughing to herself as she saw the classic one of the two walking hand-in-hand. "Who would've *possibly guessed* at that wedding that fifteen years later I'd be the one breaking the rules and you'd be so paltry that when you finally found out, all you could do was kiss my feet and drool humbly as I was walking out the door."

"If I had known that our lifestyle could've been **like this,** *I would've started fooling around on you* **years ago!"**

Kate leaned back and lazily began toying with her nipples as she swung her legs up on her husband's shoulders, digging her booted heels into his back as she squeezed her thighs against his head. Though the woman found herself overwhelmed with pleasure, she noted that it wasn't an *orgasmic pleasure* like she had grown accustomed to enjoying with Marcus … instead she felt an incredible surge of *dominance* coursing through her as she witnessed the scene that was taking place around her…

The man whom she committed to spend the rest of her days with…

…reduced to sucking the seed leftover from his unfaithful wife's lover…

…on his knees like a dog … no, **a slave…**

…and dressed up most ridiculously like a little French maid…

…all for her own amusement.

She knew that she couldn't look at him the same way after tonight, but as she felt his tongue cleaning up between her legs, it was the first time that she'd come to realize … *that she didn't have to.*

He was still her husband, as he would always be, and she still loved him deeply, and yet she also loved *to dominate him* and *to humiliate him,* and she saw herself taking a distinct pleasure in his discomfort…

...just as a real mistress would.

...just as Mistress Katherine Marie Jones **deserved!**

Kate *loved* the new woman who she was becoming. She felt sexy, and naughty, and her sex life had been elevated to something that most girls only fantasize about. But her fantasies *were* becoming very much a reality, and they were being served to her on a silver platter by none other than the humbled man who was currently licking another man's cum out of her used pussy.

And liking it...

* * * * * * * * *

The next morning, Andrew awoke to find himself in a pile of blankets on the floor beside his wife's side of the bed, still in the same vinyl maid's uniform that he'd worn the night before, with the 5" stiletto heels still buckled around his feet now causing them to be in tremendous pain while his wrists were still cuffed, though now in front of him instead of behind.

After taking a few moments to get his bearings, he looked up into the bed and found that his wife had already gotten up, then slowly took to the task of getting up onto his feet, more wobbly on the high heels than ever as he made his way across the room towards the bathroom. On his way he noticed the outfit that Kate had worn the night before – most notably her riding boots and the black leather skirt which gave him a brief flashback of kneeling in the kitchen trying to worship her ass, but being denied by the rubber gag lips that Veronica had buckled around his face to complete his feminizing costume.

Working his jaw back and forth, grateful that he hadn't also been forced to wear the gag all night long, it was then that he stepped around the corner and saw the full view of his prior night's predicament in the huge mirror on the wall … *and he didn't know quite what to think.*

The little makeup that had been left on his face had blurred and ran through the night, leaving an ugly mess combined with the fresh stubble that had grown in. Despite the brown locks that still draped quite firmly down his head, there was no denying that he looked even more ridiculous than he had last night. His wife's taunts rang in his head as he pictured her standing with her lover, laughing and pointing at the pathetic maid that he had been transformed into … yet he felt himself oddly stirring underneath his chastity belt just the same…

Andrew's wandering mind eventually focused enough to notice the note that she had left for him along with a set of keys presumably for his handcuffs on the countertop.

Free yourself and get cleaned up. Ran to the mall – be home soon.

He breathed a sigh of relief but for the first two words as he anxiously reached out to pick up the handcuff keys, then fumbled for a few moments trying to get them unlocked. The rest of the outfit was a bit more tricky and he took a surprising amount of care in removing the pins that had been holding his wig in place before then struggling to unzip the uniform from behind him, only then realizing that the entire ordeal would've been much easier had he taken a seat to remove the high heels on his feet first.

Andrew stood under the hot water in the shower for what felt like an eternity, his mind nothing but a blur of the changes that were taking place around him. All he could think about was his wife embraced with her lover, and knowing what they had done in his own living room, and then kneeling between her legs to clean up afterwards. She had grown so cavalier of her actions, and yet when he thought of her face Kate seemed sexier than ever to him.

He heard her come in the door just as he was turning off the water, and by the time he had finished toweling off she was standing there in the doorway to the bedroom holding a shopping bag from one of the department stores at the nearby mall in her outstretched hand…

"So do you want *pink* or *blue* or *purple* or *yellow* or *red???*" she asked him with a curious smile as her eyes locked onto the shiny clean steel that hung – *by her key* – between his legs.

Andrew stared blankly back at his wife, not only confused by her proposal but even more so blown away by her appearance … once again wearing something that she'd have never worn for *him* in all of their years together. The black leather pants that she wore looked like they had been painted on, highlighted by the lace-up, chunky-heeled ankle boots that he'd known of the younger, trendy girls wearing to clubs in the past. Yet his wife rocked the look like it had been made for her, wearing a simple, grey top that made nice presentation of her cleavage underneath a light jacket, and also wearing a silver necklace around her neck that he knew *he* had never given to her…

"Oh, I mean *panties!*" Kate said with a playful laugh as if he'd been in on the joke the whole time. As she reached out and handed her husband the bag, she nonchalantly explained, "These are going to be your underwear from now on – I tried to get you a variety of colors so that you can coordinate…"

The man gulped as he peered into the glossy bag and saw what was in fact a pile of women's underwear in a variety of styles and colors just as his wife had said. Reaching in to pull out a pair of lacy, purple briefs, he looked back up at his wife in shock, though he found that she had already turned to walk away, his eyes wandering to her leather-clad ass as she instructed, "Finish getting dressed and clean up in here a bit, then come see me downstairs…" while she walked away.

Though he hadn't the foggiest idea what was considered "normal" around his house anymore, Andrew felt strangely *obedient* to his wife in that very moment and after staring off into space while he fought to remove the tag, he then slipped one leg and then the other into the purple panties and carefully pulled them up over his chastity belt like it was just another day in the life.

Looking back in the mirror, he heard his wife's snickers in his head, but quickly squashed them out by telling himself that he needed to hurry and clean up so as not to keep her waiting … the vision of her in those leather pants causing him to swell considerably in his belt as he quickly finished up in the bathroom and pulled on a t-shirt and shorts before getting to work tidying up their bedroom…

Between his own outfit and the leather that Kate had worn the night before, Andrew built a sizable pile of clothes that would need to be taken out for dry cleaning, or at the very least washed personally by hand. He couldn't help but hold the skirt up to his nose as he picked it up and carried it to the pile, the scent of the leather mixing with her own aroma in a manner that just felt intoxicating to him in that very moment as he first imagined himself kneeling behind her while she wore it, then a moment later pictured his wife's lover *digging his hands into her ass through it* as he pulled her in for a tight and flagrant embrace right in front of him.

"Pretty wild night last night, huh?" she asked him as he came down the stairs to find her sitting in their breakfast nook, a small bowl of fresh fruit and her cell phone in front of her as she sipped on a mug of warm tea in her hands.

"Come sit!" Kate told him, gesturing to the chair across from her, a smile beaming across her face as if she somehow knew that *she didn't even have to ask* whether he was in fact wearing *the pretty, new panties* that she had picked up for him just that morning on a whim.

"So," she asked again with a grin as her husband's eyes wandered from a spot on the table between them to the new necklace that hung just above her bosoms, but never in the eye for longer than a split second, "what did you think of last night???"

Andrew sat there frozen for a moment while his wife studied his body language studiously, taking a few deep breaths and shifting in his seat before finally squeaking out, *"It was different."*

"It most certainly *was* different!" Kate immediately laughed amusingly in return. "Did you *enjoy* Veronica dressing you up like a little *sissy maid?!*"

Her husband stirred uncomfortably in his seat without looking up until she finally jumped back in…

"Well, I fucking *loved it!*" she told him with a boastful smile.

"The maid's uniform … the dinner … *my unexpected dinner guest* … **dessert, if you will!"**

"Can you tell that I'm still a little high right now just thinking about the whole thing?!"

Andrew looked up and met eyes with his wife, which held him for a couple of seconds longer before dropping back to the table once more.

"But do you know what *my absolute favorite part* was out of all of it, dear???" Kate then asked of her disgraced husband with a mischievous grin.

"Even more than when Marcus was *fucking me on our couch – and don't get me wrong, that by itself was* **outstanding!"** Kate admitted unabashedly, still smiling as her husband would look up and then drop his head down as he fought to understand the emotions around him.

"My *favorite* part," Kate continued, "was when we were upstairs afterwards, and you were on your knees, *and you were* **eating his cream pie out of me** … *it was such a beautiful sight to see…"*

The woman gazed out the window between them, as if

in deep contemplation as she took a long sip of her tea, before she finally leaned in a little closer, lowered her voice, and asked seductively of her husband…

"So how did he … taste???"

She raised her eyebrows with a grin as she hovered close like a vulture awaiting its next feast. When Andrew failed to answer after a few seconds passed, Kate giggled and added playfully, "Well, *I already know what he tastes like,* but I want to hear *your perspective on it…"*

Reaching out with her index finger to raise his eyes to lock with hers, Kate reiterated her demand in no uncertain terms, *"I want to know what* **my husband** *thought of the taste of* **my lover's cum** *as he was licking it* **from his wife's pussy."**

Andrew felt his heart continuing to race as he sat across from the woman he loved, emasculated in seemingly every possible way … *at least that he could imagine so far* … until Kate finally got tired of his silence and sat back as she crossed her legs and pointed down to the leather boots on her feet…

"Then why don't you get down on your knees and *worship*

me until you're ready to answer my question."

The stern tone in her voice seemed to rouse something in the speechless man and before he knew it, Andrew found himself kneeling on the tile floor next to his wife's chair, her booted foot tangling in front of his face while the scent of her leather footwear and jeans immediately sent him into overdrive as he leaned forward and brought his lips to the toe of the designer boots that he didn't recall her owning before…

Kate smiled warmly to herself as she glanced down to see her husband obediently in his place, then took another sip from her mug before she began to muse out loud to herself as much as to her budding submissive husband's audience at her feet…

"I think the reason that I enjoyed that view so much…" she began whimsically, *"is because in that one perfect moment, it confirmed for me something of the utmost importance about you that has been on my mind ever since we started down this road."*

"By seeing you in that **vulnerable state,** *put* **completely** *at my mercy and* **willing to submit** *to my most* **carnal desires,"** she continued as she looked down once more to savor the

image of Andrew's lips hard at work on the leather around her feet.

"It proved to me that my husband is willing to do **ANYTHING** *for me … no matter how depraved, no matter how humiliating … if it's something that will bring me pleasure."*

"And that makes me **very happy,** *slave,"* she spoke, the word *slave* seeming to just roll off of her tongue as if it was completely natural.

It was then that Kate abruptly stood up from her chair, reaching down and grabbing her husband's hair and forcing his face into her crotch as she snarled at him to place his wrists behind his back.

"I know that these last few months have been rather demanding on you…" she continued as she rubbed Andrew's nose against the tight leather separating him from her sex.

"…and to be honest, I don't necessarily think that it's going to *stop* anytime soon."

"I'm having far too much fun with my new lifestyle – *fucking Marcus, being served by you …* what kind of girl in her right mind would give a good thing like that up?!"

"So I'm glad that you're starting to learn to *accept* this twist that our relationship has turned *because I really have no desire to turn back now!*"

"Besides," she said with a laugh as she shook her head staring down at him, *"look at you!* You might not be able to put it into words, *but you're on cloud 9 having me stand over you in leather right now!* You'd probably cum in a heartbeat if it wasn't for, well, *I guess that's the price you pay for getting to play this little game with me…"*

Kate made a few humping motions towards her husband's face before releasing his hair and pushing him backwards before lunging forward and climbing on top of him, straddling him as she leaned in with her lips an inch from his face.

"Now I'm going to ask you **again…"** she growled as she pinned his wrists down over his head while she stared coercively into his eyes.

"What did my lover's cum taste like … **on your lips** *… as you were dutifully sucking it out of my pussy???"*

Andrew lay there frozen as his wife sat on top of him with all of her might, his mouth dry with the lingering taste of boot leather, his beautiful dominant only an inch away with her demands. He couldn't help but notice that she seemed more radiant than ever, even in the position that she had put him in … possibly *because of* the position that she had put him in … and so after what seemed like yet another eternity had passed, he finally opened his mouth and squeaked out the response that shocked even himself…

"It tasted … delicious…" he stammered.

"…because it tasted … **like you."**

Kate smirked in surprise as she stared down at her husband, "Oh really?!"

"Yes," he sheepishly nodded. *"You haven't had sex with me in such a long while, I guess I'll take whatever taste of you I can get…"*

Kate laughed as she read the submission in his eyes and fed off of it even more.

"Even if it's **cleaning up** *after my lover has ravished me in ways that you never could???"*

Andrew paused and then slowly nodded, his eyes locked with those of his wife.

"Even if it's just **kissing my boots** *before I go out for a night of debauchery and leave you behind to do all of the chores???"*

Andrew gulped and nodded quietly once more as the woman breathed down his face.

"Good!" she exclaimed suddenly as she leaned forward and gave him a quick peck on the lips before jumping up from her throne and announcing, "Marcus wanted me to meet him for lunch today, so now that you're finally up, *you can drive me."*

* * * * * * * * * *

Kate sat in the passenger seat of their SUV playing on her phone as Andrew drove to the address of the small bistro where his wife would be meeting her boyfriend for lunch. Though the two hadn't spoken a word since she had let him up from the kitchen floor, a strange calm fell over Andrew as if maybe *he was* learning to accept the new role that he had taken in his wife's life…

Slipping a pair of sexy, oversized sunglasses on as he pulled up to the curb in front of the restaurant, Kate nonchalantly told him, "Come around and open my door for me," as she slipped her phone into her purse.

Feeling a bit haughty as Andrew walked around the car without argument and held her door while she emerged like a movie star from her escort, Kate then waited for him to close the door behind him before informing him, "I'll probably be out for most of the afternoon, so I'll just take a cab or have Marcus drive me home afterwards."

"What are your plans?" Andrew asked calmly as he stared back into his wife's tinted lenses.

"I don't know," she told him with a non-committal shrug. Seeing her reflection in the glass of the building nearby, she prodded with a giggle, "He'll probably want to show me off for a little, so maybe we'll go to the museum or stop by the winery before heading back to his place." She toyed with the silver necklace as she spoke, which upon closer inspection he saw was in a heart shape with diamond accents.

Upon noticing his glances, Kate took a step closer to her husband and held out the charm freely as she asked with a smile, "Do you like it? *Marcus gave it to me as a 3-month anniversary gift…"*

She gloated at the sucker-punched look on his face, then twisted the knife a bit further as she leaned in and whispered, *"You know that we're probably going to* **fuck** *some more when we get back to his place, right???"*

Andrew hung on the seductive woman's every word as he looked back into her piercing eyes and nodded, "Yes. Of course…"

Kate laughed, her body almost but not quite pressing up against his, adding, *"Do you want me to bring you anything?!"*

Andrew gulped and cleared his throat.

"If you'd like…"

"We'll see – maybe if you're a good boy," she snickered as she stepped back and then sized up her husband as he stood before her. After pausing to consider her latest thought for a moment, she added, "I think if you're going to start *serving me* more regularly, it's time that you started being more *professional* about it."

"You clean my clothes, you cook my meals, you drove me here," Kate explained, "so it seems only proper that you would *address me* as a lady's servant would as well."

Andrew looked back at his wife confused until she finally prompted him…

"Call me **Mistress Katherine."**

"Mistress Katherine?"

"Again."

"Yes, Mistress Katherine…" his eyes falling to the sidewalk as the new moniker fell from his lips.

"From now on, that's what you call me," she spoke astutely. "Kate, Katie, Katherine … those are names for *other people* now. **My slave** *calls me Mistress Katherine* … is that understood?"

Her husband bit his lip as he considered her tone and complied, "Yes, Mistress Katherine…"

"Good!" she confirmed with a satisfied smile. "Now get down and kiss my boot goodbye so that I can go enjoy lunch with my boyfriend.”

Andrew paused and looked around, but was immediately confronted for his delay.

“Yes, in front of all of these people,” she scolded him as she tapped her boot against the concrete. “Are you ashamed to be seen worshipping your Mistress?!”

Her husband frowned, then shook his head and looked back at the ground in the direction of her feet.

“Then do it.”

Kate rolled her eyes at his discomfort as she watched him take a deep breath, then bend down on his knees near her feet. Looking around herself, curious if she had any other admirers, she corrected him once more just before he reached her toes, *“Back of the heel — don’t linger.”*

Andrew blushed as he craned his neck to reach around to the back of his wife’s boot, then brought his lips to the designer leather on her heel before quickly standing back up in hopes of not attracting any attention. As he glanced around after dusting himself off, Kate took a step closer and asked authoritatively, “Don’t you have something to tell me now?"

Andrew looked at the woman across from him, her sparkling eyes shielded by her sunglasses, then looked down her body and back – leather pants and all. *She looked like a goddess,* and spying the tiny nook on the back of her heel where he had just knelt down to pay her tribute, he'd never felt more humbled.

Under his shorts, he wore a steel chastity belt to which this woman possessed the only key … and as he looked back into her presence, he felt the bizarre sensation of actually wishing that she would engage the spikes just so that he could see it please her right in that very moment.

He heard himself say the words out loud to her without even realizing that he was saying them…

"Thank you for letting me kiss your boots, Mistress Katherine. I hope you have a good afternoon with your lover."

Kate turned her head and smiled, then snickered, "Thanks, cucky – I'm sure that I will!"

As she then turned to walk away, Kate heard her husband add, "What would you like me to do while you're gone,

Mistress Katherine?"

Without turning back, knowing that his eyes would be firmly locked on her ass in the super sexy leather jeans, Kate simply shouted over her shoulder, *"I don't know - surprise me!"* as she walked away towards the restaurant.

Andrew stood there beside the car and watched his wife eventually disappear into the bistro, unable to see her embrace when she finally met up with her lover but picturing it in his mind from the past night's recollection just the same. His hands would dig in and cradle her butt in perfectly crafted leather, she would lean in to him like her body was molded specifically for his, and then the two would kiss … not like a married couple kisses, or even like a lust-filled pair who had just started dating … *a naughtier type of kiss … one that was meant* **to tease** *just as much as it was meant* **to titillate.**

Andrew pictured his wife in this embrace with her lover, him appearing insignificantly at her feet, reduced to kissing only the bottoms of the sexy ankle boots that she wore for him while she flaunted her affair in his face. Eventually she would blindfold him so that he was unable to watch, and as he listened he would hear her too succumbing to whatever kinky desires were planned for her before ultimately Marcus would tower over his wife and take her pussy once again as his own.

He imagined her legs spread wide as he was then instructed to *do his job* and come in behind her lover to clean up his mess, his wife laughing with each lick until Marcus finally shoved him aside and told him to wait in the corner while he returned to claiming the woman once more.

It wasn't until a car behind him waiting to drop off its own guests honked that Andrew suddenly snapped out of his unexpected fantasy, walked back around to the driver's side of the SUV, and pulled away. His cock stirring desperately inside of its cage, the whole way home his mind flooded with ways to surprise his mistress when she would return later that day…

* * * * * * * * *

"I like just *being with you,*" Kate confessed to Marcus as the two walked hand in hand down the long, marble hall of the museum, her chunky-heeled boots echoing through the chamber with each step to her own amusement. "I'm kind of glad that I think Andrew is slowly learning to …

embrace our new lifestyle, so hopefully we'll be able to start spending a little more time together!"

"But it's really important that *he* gets something out of this, too…" she added as they made their way around the corner towards the main exhibition hall.

"Of course!" her lover replied with a hearty laugh as the two walked. "It's not really *cuckolding* if the husband doesn't find his own reward from the relationship … otherwise it would just be *you cheating on him.*"

Kate smiled softly.

"Yeah … it just still amazes me that this all came about so fast," she admitted. "It seems like one minute you were flirting with me over lunch at work and the next we were picking out chastity belts for my husband!"

The two laughed together at the thought.

"Like I've told you," Marcus continued contently, "it's all just about timing. I was *eager,* you were *curious,* he was … *obedient!* Each of us just happened to be in the perfect place at the perfect time, *and here we are…*"

Kate leaned in and stole a brief kiss with a giggle.

"So I wonder what he's doing right now…" she mused as they began to walk casually among the exhibits as if they were just another couple out for a lazy afternoon of wandering.

"What would *you* like for him to be doing right now???" Marcus posed back to her inquisitively.

Without hesitation or modesty, Kate almost immediately shot back, "I want him to be thinking about *worshipping* me. And *serving* me."

"I swear, I could walk around feeling like this *every day* and it would suit me just fine!" she added with a grin as she looked back at her lover confidently.

"Well you **do** *look mighty fine in* **leather,** *that's for sure!"* Marcus complimented her with a wide smile as he looked her up and down and then reached down and unabashedly grabbed her ass in public.

"Thank you!" she purred loudly as she swatted back at him playfully. "I *feel* fine in this, and for some reason knowing how much it makes his jaw drop that *he can't have* *me in this* makes it feel *that much sexier!* I could wear this stuff every day if you bought it for me…"

"I just might," the tall man shot back with a mischievous smile.

As the two rounded the next corner in the hall, they came upon the special exhibition that had compelled Marcus to bring Kate to the museum that day in the first place…

PLEASURE AND RESTRAINTS THROUGHOUT HISTORY

…read the sign that hung overhead as a sly grin drifted across Kate's burgundy lips.

"What's *this???*" she asked seductively as she squeezed a little closer to her man as the two approached.

Marcus smiled.

"I thought you might enjoy this … *on a number of different levels,*" he explained coolly as he produced the special entry tickets from his pocket and handed them over to the attendant as they walked past. "Apparently it's been very *controversial* for how *graphic* it is, but the people who are really into this sort of stuff all say that it's an *incredibly thorough* display…"

As they walked into the first room to find the layout of a professional dungeon, complete with restraints hanging from the wall and a padded spanking bench, Marcus then added eagerly, "And did I mention that all of the exhibits happen to be *hands on?*"

Kate grinned as she walked into the otherwise empty room and slid her bare hand across the spanking bench, imagining someone … *or herself* … knelt on the padded bench … *or bound to it* … awaiting their punishment … *or pleasure…*

"Climb up!" Marcus told her as he walked up beside, clearly impressed himself with the *opportunity* that the unique museum exhibits had to offer.

"Someone will see!" Kate protested as she continued to eye the bench, imagining it between her thighs and wishing that it could be more…

"No — they won't," Marcus insisted as he placed a hand firmly on her leather-clad ass and guided her accordingly. "The

exhibits are all private," he explained. "See those lights by the door? They change from red to green when whoever's in the next room has moved on, and they only let enough people through to have one group in each section at a time."

"Really…?" Kate confirmed with an aroused smirk before leaning into her lover and kissing him passionately in the center of the dungeon. When their kiss finally broke, she turned seductively and looked behind her at him as she lifted one knee up onto the bench, then swung her other leg over, scooting up until she was straddling the red padding with her feet at one end and her hands and head at the other.

"Beautiful!" Marcus exclaimed as he obligatorily slapped the woman's ass as the bench positioned it perfectly for his viewing pleasure, eliciting a playful yelp as he then reached down and buckled the cuffs at one end around each of her booted ankles before moving forward to apply the same to her wrists, followed by a much larger strap that laid across her back and ensured without a doubt that she wouldn't be getting up until he allowed her to…

"Now you see, *the beauty* of a spanking bench like this," he explained to her as he relocated back around behind her, "is that it's great *for spanking…*" which he then illustrated with a few more well-placed smacks that caused Kate to grunt with desire.

"Or alternatively…" he continued as he moved in closer between her legs and bumped his crotch between them, "you'll notice that you *also* happen to be in a wonderful position *for something else…"*

Kate began rubbing back against her captor as much as her bondage would allow, looking up at the mirror that had been strategically placed in front of her to see her lover prepared to mount her proudly from behind. She groaned in frustration as she thought she could feel Marcus's cock through his jeans and wished that he could just pull down her pants and take her right then and there, but instead he soon walked around back to her head – not to release her, but to show her how the bench also positioned *her head* seemingly perfectly should he desire to put her succulent lips to work instead.

"You think we can get one of these for your apartment?!" she purred out in desperation as she begged to be touched by her lover in pretty much any way.

Marcus just chuckled as he circled around her, enjoying the desirable, new predicament that his sexy companion now found herself in…

"Just think, if we *did,* I could just leave you bound to this thing *all night long!*" he laughed, running a hand along the back of her thigh, admiring how the black leather stretched exquisitely over the woman's firmly toned legs. "And whenever I wanted some more, *I could just walk by* **and take it,** *and there's nothing you could do to stop me…*"

"Who's to say that I'd want to stop you?!" she jeered back with a giggle. *"What kind of a slut would I be for my man if my body wasn't available to him whenever he wanted it?"*

"Speaking of sluts…" Marcus murmured as he made his rounds once more, then spotting Kate's purse sitting nearby and finding a new idea to add a bit more spice to their day. Just out of his bound woman's line of sight, Marcus retrieved Kate's cell phone from the top of her purse and a moment later he was once again towering behind her, first taking a photo of the woman's ass lifted gloriously into the air on its own and then posing for a second photo himself that showed him much closer, as if he was penetrating the bound woman from behind as he'd teased her about earlier…

"Hey – what's going on back there?!" Kate asked playfully as she strained to see behind her before Marcus appeared once again by her side a moment later, her phone still in hand.

"Oh, I just thought it might be fun to take a few pictures of the lady to send home to her husband…" he snickered as he held up the phone so that she could see his work.

"God, my ass looks good in these!" she remarked at the first picture, then adding, *"That one looks yummy…"* in response to the next.

"Here, now get one with me blowing you…" she then prompted as she lifted her head and opened her lips in the classic position while her lover pressed his crotch into her face and then leaned back to pose with Kate's obscured and her wrists in shackles framing up another iconic shot.

It was just before Marcus was tempted to break the rules and unzip his pants – *even if just for a few seconds* – when a buzzer rang in their room that prompted them to move forward so that the next visitors could enter the room that they were currently enjoying. Kate immediately fell into his arms once she had been freed, her leg riding up firmly against his manhood while her tongue danced with his passionately to show that she had *really* enjoyed her time being bound for him…

Throughout the rest of the display, the two continued to push the limits of *hands on* a bit more than most of the other visitors browsing the exhibit as the couple took every opportunity to add another kinky pose to Kate's growing album documenting her own submission. The next hour found Kate with her wrists in steel shackles over her head like a damsel in distress, locked up tight in a leather straitjacket that seemed to be designed to perfectly match the rest of her leather ensemble, and even spread out taut on a torture rack with her body pulled in every direction … *which lead to a rather provocative photo of Marcus* **slipping his hand down her pants** *in a manner that should've required her* **being gagged** *as well.*

In addition to her own captivity, however, the married woman wasn't without her own ideas as she also noted a number of contraptions that she could already see lending themselves to her domination of her own budding slave during the times when she wasn't herself helplessly captive to her strong and imposing lover. She marveled at the display showing the history of chastity belts throughout the years and noted that alongside what they had centuries ago, in reality the model her husband had been forced into *wasn't really that bad by comparison!*

She also toured a variety of spanking and discipline implements – many of which brought *a special tingle* when she held them in her hands and imagined Andrew on his hands and knees with a bright red ass before her, but what *really* caught her eye was a device in the form of a cage that had been built into the underside of a queen-size bed, thus further reinforcing the separation of *a lady and her slave* in a way that left her feeling particularly hot and bothered inside…

"He *did* sleep on the floor beside my bed last night," Kate found her telling Marcus as if to sell him or seek his approval for the dominant step. "I cuffed his hands in front of him instead of behind him so that he wouldn't hurt himself, and then I fell asleep *touching myself thinking of you* while he slept beneath me…"

Marcus smirked as he leaned over to admire the sturdy construction of the steel bars below the bed.

"Well, it would be a rather *bold step* in terms of tease and denial," he commented. "He doesn't get to *touch you* very much these days anymore anyways, does he?"

An unexpected smile slipped its way across Kate's face…

"No…" she replied. "He mainly keeps to my legs and feet, and I think I actually like it when he kisses *my shoes* because I feel like that way I'm denying him even those … but last night when he cleaned up after you was the first time that he was really near my pussy since he's been locked up."

Marcus turned her to face him as they both sat down on the corner of the cage bed.

"And do you like that?" he asked the woman openly as he stared into her deep brown eyes.

Kate paused and seriously thought for a moment, then looked back at him and replied, *"I* **really** *do!"*

"I feel like this gives me the best of both worlds," Kate explained as she held her lover's hand in her own. *"I get more intimacy out of* **dominating** *my husband than I ever did before, and then I've got* **you** *to fill in the gaps that he's leaving behind falling into this new role …* **and then some!"**

"Sometimes I just wonder if we're going to hit a breaking point where he's finally going to say **no**, but…" she trailed off, deep in thought.

"But what?" Marcus prodded her to continue as he pulled her a little closer as they slid back into the center of the luxuriously large, leather-lined bed.

"…but then I look back at the things that *I've already done to him*, and … I don't know … I guess I just *honestly don't see him putting up a fight…*"

"I think I might actually have him in the palm of my hand, to where I could pretty much do *anything I want to him…*" Kate spoke more softly as she placed her hand on his chest.

"*…just like* **a real slave…**"

With her final word, Kate climbed onto her lover and madly stuck her tongue down his throat, overcome with passion as everything seemed to avalanche in one sexually-charged triumph. The pair wrestled playfully as she scrambled to finish her erotic thought between breaths…

"And then my body takes over, and I forget that he's my husband, and I just want to push him lower and lower … **just to see how**

far down he'll go for me."

"And it makes me SO WET just thinking about BEING SO NASTY to him, *and a part of me says that* **it's not normal** *and that I need to quit…"*

"…but then I've got him at my feet … **in public** *… thanking me for letting him give the tiniest of kisses to my boots … before I say goodbye to go off and* **fuck another man…"**

"And it makes me feel like a goddess … so powerful, so desirable…"

"And does this goddess keep her servants locked up in cages when they're not in use???" Marcus egged her on as he groped her breasts and crotch before flipping her onto her back in the center of the padded bed.

"I think she does," Kate cooed as she watched her lover then reach for the Velcro straps built into the mattress and quickly fasten her wrists above her head, then a moment later apply similar straps around her ankles as well, spreading her legs in the process as she lay there exposed and invigorated.

"How do you think he'll feel when he's *locked underneath in his cage* and he can hear his goddess *getting tied down and fucked*

just a few inches above his head?!" Marcus growled at her as he laid his body on top of hers and began biting passionately at her neck.

"He'll feel like he's lucky to be in the same room as me as I'm being pleasured ... **if he knows what's good for him!"** she groaned as she struggled deliciously against her bonds, waiting to feel him penetrate her and forgetting entirely that they were still in a public setting there at the museum.

"I think you've got more of that *nasty bitch* in you than you think!" Marcus laughed as he slowed his advances, catching his breath as he stared down at the woman beneath him, bound so breathtaking and succulent.

Kate snarled as she enjoyed the pressure of Marcus's hand over her leather crotch a moment longer, joking, "Baby, I thought that it *turned you on* when I was *cruel* to my husband…"

Marcus leaned in to kiss her, his hands still holding her wrists in place over the simple, but effective Velcro restraints.

"You know it does…" he confirmed as he nibbled

passionately on her lips, eventually leaning back to take a couple of pictures of the sexy woman bound on her back for the collection before finally freeing her just before the buzzer rang to herd them towards the exit of the exhibit.

"Before we leave, get a picture of the cage, too," Kate prompted as she slid to the edge of the bed after her lover, dangling her boots provocatively in front of the cage door as she posed for a picture that her imagination knew could quite easily become a daily ritual. She had already said it once before – it was *her* bed, not *their* bed … and the thought of denying him just one more thing made her giddy with excitement as she jumped off the magnificent bondage device and took her beau's hand in hers once more as they walked out of the exhibit, soon thereafter deciding to leave the rest of the museum behind to make a bee-line to Marcus's apartment instead to pick up where the two had fervidly left off…

* * * * * * * * *

It was considerably later than she had planned when Kate finally walked back in her own front door after spending the remainder of the afternoon as well as most of the evening in the arms of her lover or tied to his bed with the silk ties that he had just introduced to her that night, much to her enjoyment.

The house was already dark save for some ambient lighting that Andrew must've left on for her before going to bed, though she was impressed just the same when she stepped into the kitchen and came to find the bountiful display of goodies that she figured must've kept him busy all day gathering for her while she was away. Around a beautiful bouquet of color flowers were placed a number of gift boxes and envelopes that she slowly dug through one by one:

An envelope containing a gift card for a one-hour massage at the spa nearby...

Another containing a gift certificate for her to get her hair and nails done...

A shoe box that held a very stylish pair of deep brown, strappy leather sandals that she almost immediately pictured her husband worshipping on a bright summer's day...

Another box — this one far more sinister — containing a heavy leather paddle that she imagined he must've picked up at the local sex store and that seemed to fit in her hand just perfectly…

And last but not least, one final envelope – the contents of which made her eyes water as she sat down to read it, still caressing the leather paddle with her free hand. Inside the envelope was a letter written on a single lined piece of paper, handwritten in what seemed to be the most perfect penmanship that her husband could've possibly mustered word after word, line after line. The letter itself read:

My Dear Mistress Katherine,

Since the day upon which I first met you, my only goal has been to make you happy – through sickness and in health, in the name of our marriage and all that I honor in life … whatever makes you happy, makes me happy.

It's taken me time to understand and accept this new turn that our lives together have taken, yet with each day seeing the passion in your heart grow I find myself able to tolerate the pain a little more. The pain is a challenge for me to be my best for you, and I want to prove that I can take all that you have to give me.

I love you more every day and that hasn't stopped even with these new desires you've found … in whatever capacity you choose, my

Kate paced around her living room with tears in her eyes, but extraordinarily happy as she read the words that her husband had left for her over and over again, elated for this new breakthrough in his acceptance of her lifestyle if albeit temporarily taken aback in the position of dominance that she was to hold over his head.

Pouring herself a glass of wine, she sat back down at the island and poured over her gifts again, slowly slipping back into her prior state of mind and allowing herself to be bolstered by his testimony instead of taken aback by it. As she caressed the paddle in her hands and admired the rich leather heels and even planned out in her head when she could make use of the spa and salon treatments in the week to come, her mind also drifted back to Andrew at her feet, begging for scraps of her affection while she flaunted her infidelity with great delight.

When she finally did walk up the stairs to their bedroom, Kate was surprised one step further to find Andrew not sound asleep on his side of the bed per usual, but instead very much as she had left him the night before … curled up in a pile of blankets, admittedly this time much more comfortably, off to one side of the bed, with his wrists even handcuffed in front of him as before and the bright purple panties which she had picked out for him at the mall earlier that morning nestled snugly around his shiny and secure steel chastity belt…

Making her best effort not to disturb him as she crept into the closet to slip out of the leather that had helped her to shine all day long, Kate soon found herself laying in bed alone with one hand between her legs and another playing with her nipple, fantasizing about taking her lover's cock between her lips while her slave lay sound asleep on the floor below her.

Though she had left Marcus's an hour prior with some *very exciting* news that she couldn't wait to tell him, Kate let out a soft moan as she conceded to holding that new surprise until they both awoke in the morning…

* * * * * * * * *

Andrew arose the next day to find his wife asleep in the

bed above him, unsure of what time she had actually returned home after spending the bulk of the day with her boyfriend. After slipping downstairs to confirm that she had in fact opened the gifts that he had left out for her, he then settled into his morning routine of first cleaning himself up in the bathroom … *coupled with selecting a new pair of panties to wear that day,* and then organizing Kate's dirty clothes and putting her boots away from the previous day before returning to the kitchen to begin preparing tea and breakfast for them both to share.

Kate smiled warmly when she appeared from the hallway wearing a silky red robe and matching marabou slippers, taking the fresh mug from her place at the table as she greeted her husband…

"Thank you for the lovely tribute last night…" she applauded him, glancing back over at the flowers and gifts that were still piled high in the center of the kitchen island for her. "It was a *very nice* surprise for me to come home to find."

"You're welcome," Andrew replied from his place in front of the stove. "I'm glad that you enjoyed them."

"And thank *you,*" he then added with a hint of anxiety in his voice, "for *the photos* that you shared from your day yesterday…"

Kate grinned.

"I'm glad you liked them!" she said with a quiet laugh, thinking back to the handful of kinky photos they had taken throughout the museum exhibit the other day as well as those that she had elected *not to send him.*

"Did it *turn you on* seeing your mistress all bound and helpless like that?" she asked with a coy chuckle as she sipped from her tea.

Andrew murmured a simple, *"Maybe…"* as he walked over to her side and slid a plate in front of her before returning to the stove, which prompted his wife to invite him to sit down.

"Come – make yourself a plate and sit down, and then I want to hear *a real answer* to my question," she told him emphatically. "Nobody gets *kind of* aroused – either something turns you on or it doesn't!"

"Did it turn *you* on?" Andrew asked cautiously as he

filled his own plate and then took the chair opposite his wife, already knowing the answer yet both nervous and somewhat excited to hear the words from her mouth at the same time.

"Very much so!" Kate grinned, pausing to reflect as she twirled a bite of egg on her fork. "I liked having my *wrists and ankles bound* and being unable to resist his advances … just as much as I liked *being photographed,* knowing that you would be back at home *writhing in your chastity belt* as each voyeuristic depiction popping up on your phone!"

Amused by the blushed look that was creeping across her husband's face, she then added, *"Is that something you'd like for me to do for you again in the future?"*

Andrew swallowed hard on his next bite before looking up to meet her question with a simple nod.

"Ok, then I'll see what I can do…" Kate chimed brightly as she smiled back at him approvingly.

"So anyways, what I wanted to talk to you about this morning," Kate then segued in between bites of the delicious omelet that Andrew had prepared for her, "is that

I'm actually rather glad that you enjoyed shopping for me yesterday because I think I'm going to send you out to get a few things for me today, too…"

"You see, Marcus wants to take me out of town next weekend, and he thought that I should have some new clothes for our trip."

Taken a bit off guard by the new proposition of his wife traveling with her lover, Andrew fumbled a bit as he asked her, "So … where were you planning to go???"

"Vegas," she replied with a sleek grin. "I've always wanted to go and Marcus seems to think that we could have a lot of fun there, so he's going to make plans for us to fly out for a long weekend there together. He's been under a lot of stress at work lately, so he really wants to make a big deal out of it – *first class airfare, a gorgeous hotel suite, the nightlife…"*

"And so we both agreed that my wardrobe could use a little *sprucing up* to live up to the rest of the trip," Kate explained while her husband sat awkwardly across from her absorbing her latest plans.

"I was thinking maybe a nice evening dress, a couple of sexy cocktail dresses for dancing, something nice and skimpy to wear by the pool

… and of course, I'll need some new **high heels and lingerie** *to go with it all…"*

Andrew struggled to clear something in his throat before he could respond…

"Mistress Katherine, with all due respect," he told his wife, "I'm not sure if we can afford all of that right now." He bit his lip and looked down, waiting for the blowback, but instead Kate simply got up from the table and walked over to retrieve her purse that she had been using the day before.

"Don't worry," she told him with a grin as she sat back down at the table and pulled a small envelope out of her purse, sliding it across the table towards him. "It's already taken care of…"

"What's this?" he asked as he opened the envelope to find a hundred dollar bill staring back at him … a considerable number of them when he pulled them out and splayed the crisp bills out on the table next to his breakfast plate.

"There should be $5,000 there … *but let me know if it's not enough and I can get more…"* Kate told her husband nonchalantly as she took another sip from her tea.

"But where???" he stuttered confused.

"I told you – Marcus wants our weekend together to be *perfect,* and he knows that we can't afford the types of clothes that he likes to see me in on your salary."

"There's enough here to **pay off our car!"** he exclaimed flabbergasted.

"I know…" Kate simply replied with a chuckle, *"but instead, it's going to buy me a couple of pairs of shoes and some underwear fitting of a high class lady like myself visiting Las Vegas with her boyfriend for the first time!"*

"And get some more **leather,** *too,"* she added with an evil grin. *"Leather seems to really drive my boyfriend wild …* **and me, too."**

"There should be some boutiques in **the expensive mall** *that will have what you're looking for."*

"Again, call me if you don't have enough – I want this to be **perfect."**

∗ ∗ ∗ ∗ ∗ ∗ ∗ ∗ ∗

His shopping trip was one like no other as he walked

nervously around the mall that was typically *way* out of his price range with the money of his wife's lover funding his visit. He felt the awkward tension with each store that he walked into as he told the clerks that he was there shopping for his wife, knowing in the back of his head what the real intentions of her new wardrobe additions were to be only a few short days away…

Of course, it certainly didn't help that Kate had engaged the spikes inside of his chastity belt to their second of four settings … *"to keep him focused while he was shopping for his mistress."*

He found the lingerie stores to be the most demanding of him, although the stores selling sensually high heels were a close second … perhaps because those were two fetishes that seemed to put him on edge as he browsed their aisles the most. To peruse the sexy straps and provocative designs that would serve to excite both his wife and her lover was overwhelming as he pictured both Kate slipping into them like a tease on the prowl and then Marcus later tearing them back off of her like an animal claiming its prize.

Her request for leather had him a bit stumped until he happened across a store that seemed to specialize in the most daunting of fashions, its racks filled with skirts and bustiers and long, leather ball gowns that boasted price tags exceeded his entire budget for a single dress. Though it took some careful selection to ensure that he could fulfill each of the items that his wife had requested, he made certain to leave a few bills appropriately to purchase the longline leather corset that he pictured cinching his wife's already perfect figure into one which he could only imagine…

…*the perfect corset to be worshipped,* **or to worship someone else in…**

On his drive back to the house after many long hours of humiliating shopping for his mistress, the smells of leather and perfumes teasing him all the more as they wafted throughout the car, Andrew's mind continued to drift between the domineering, new corset that he had just purchased and the special photos that Kate had sent him from her *little adventure* the afternoon before. Though he had spent almost the entirety of the money that she had given to him between the multitude of designer boxes that now filled the trunk of the car, he nonetheless found himself making one last stop to help his wife embrace her kinky tendencies before finally returning home.

It become instantly clear that Kate was quite impressed with her husband's shopping efforts as she first watched him parade load after load of boxes from the car up to their bedroom, then joined him for her own personal tour as he walked her through his purchases one by one.

Her eyes lit up with a devious glint when they reached the lingerie and she saw the glamorously sexy arrangements of silk and lace that he had bought to adorn her body in the most intimate of settings, though her reaction to the leather corset as she held it alluringly up to her figure was second only to the final purchases that Andrew had saved for last that he had purchased for her with his own money…

Leather wrist and ankle cuffs, black with stunning purple highlights, a matching leather blindfold, and even a bright purple ballgag.

Running her fingers across the beautifully hand-stitched leather, eyeing the purple accents in her favorite color … deep down she knew that *these toys* weren't intended for her to use on her husband.

Andrew had bought them **for Marcus to use on her.**

Overwhelmed with emotion once more at her husband's

latest display of understanding, Kate thanked him wholeheartedly and then asked for some privacy so that she could try on some of her new clothes by herself. When she finally reached the leather corset, Kate went all out and retrieved a fresh pair of black stockings, her stiletto boots, and spent twenty minutes primping her hair and makeup before returning to the bed where her new bondage cuffs were all that remained…

The leather smooth and inviting, it didn't take long for her to buckle each of the four restraints around her wrists and ankles, and even slip the purple ballgag tight between her shiny, inviting lips. As she looked in the mirror back at herself, she saw that all that was left to complete the outfit was a black and purple collar locked around her neck.

…but she knew that **her husband** *wasn't the appropriate person to make* **that purchase** *for her…*

First posing for a few photos that she would later send over to Marcus, she then stretched out on the bed and reached over into her nightstand to retrieve the realistic silicone dildo that called home the top drawer. Eventually pulling the blindfold too down over her eyes, too, it took little effort for Kate to slip the 8-1/2" long replica of her lover deep inside, her soft moans against the gag an entirely new sensation as she stretched her body wide and imagined her wrists and ankles clipped to the corners of the bed like they had been in the museum exhibit the other day.

…in and out, the dildo thrust between her legs as she begged for his any touch…

…her husband in chains in his cage below them, desperate for every breath of passion that her muffled lips squeaked out…

She allowed herself to buck against the dildo three separate times before finally committing that she would wait until her vacation when she knew that Marcus would be more than happy to tie her aching body down to the bed and tease her relentlessly for real.

Each night for the following week, Kate and Andrew followed the same routine – they would start with foot and shoe worship as Kate flirted on the phone with her man; then upon her satisfaction, she would put her new paddle to good use, giving her husband's ass as many spanks as she desired on a given day; and then finally, the day would end with one more step in preparation for her trip, be it *packing her suitcase, shaving her legs, shaving* **other areas** *specifically for a* *special someone…*

Everything was changing so quickly, but Kate couldn't bear for it to slow down in the slightest. As Andrew continued to take every new thing that she threw at him, she still wondered if one day she would unwittingly come across his breaking point, but until that day each step down for him was simply another step for her to dominantly ascend.

Of course, neither of them had any idea what to expect when it was time for Kate to board her flight to Vegas merely a week later…

Also Available from KinkyWriter Erotic Media…

Collections & Samplers

<u>New Beginnings - a collection of Kinky Erotica, vol. 1</u>

Featuring 18 kinky adventures spanning topics from bondage to domination, chastity, fetishes, and even a little cuckolding…

<u>Dark Fantasies – a KinkyWriter.com erotic sampler</u>

Not every fantasy is one that we dare speak aloud, and in this collection we explore a sampling of hardcore erotica that pushes the boundaries of BDSM, cuckolding, and sadomasochism to new depths…

<u>Romantic Restraints – a KinkyWriter.com erotic sampler</u>

Romance is in the air as we explore stories of dedication and devotion, domination and discipline to make your heart a' flutter … not to mention stir certain other parts as well…

<u>Fantasies in Fetish - a sexy collection of bondage, femdom, and other naughty vignettes</u>

Sometimes it admittedly doesn't take much to get the juices flowing of your friendly, neighborhood kinksters and this collection skips the introductions and cuts straight to the chase with more erotic adventures than ever before…

The Best of KinkyWriter.com, vol. 1

A total of 10 kinky tales make up this nostalgic collection of KinkyWriter.com reader favorites – available FREE from most online retailers!

Short Stories & Novellas

One Last Tease…

Distraught over the recent breakup with his girlfriend, David finds himself on an unexpected kinky adventure with his ex- pulling all of the string…

30 Days of Bondage

He wanted to know what it would be like … to be a prisoner … to be utterly helpless … without an end in sight…

The Photo Shoot

Allison Hall pays a visit to a local dominatrix named Madame Genevieve who promises to teach her a thing or two during a special kinky photo shoot…

Enjoying My Bondage

Every passion has to start somewhere - meet Callie and let her tell you why she loves bondage as she sets the stage for even more kinky tales soon to come...

A Bitch's Makeover

Maria knew that there was no one who could teach her how to be a bitch like her friend Shannon could…

Her Greatest Weakness

Jessica was normally a mild-mannered, happily married girl, but when he came calling from her past, she knew from the moment she heard his voice that she was powerless to resist…

About the Author

KinkyWriter has been writing BDSM and fetish erotica for more than a decade, sharing their fine appreciation for the decadent details about leather and latex, bondage and restraints, domination and submission, and so much more!

Did you enjoy the stories that you just read here today?

Visit KinkyWriter.com for hundreds of erotic adventures covering all sorts of your favorite kinky topics, including:

bondage · domination · chastity · fetishes

crossdressing · spanking · humiliation · masturbation

discipline · tease & denial · latex · CBT · high heels

leather · role playing · submission · electroplay

cuckolding · hypnosis · forced orgasms · isolation

Follow along on your favorite social media sites to ensure that you never miss a single naughty story!

- **Twitter** – https://twitter.com/kinky_writer

- **Instagram** – https://instagram.com/kinky_writer

- **Pinterest –** https://pinterest.com/kinkywriter

Subscribe to KinkyWriter on Patreon for access to sneak peeks of upcoming releases, exclusive vignettes not published anywhere else, and the **KinkyWriter Story Vault** – filled with dozens and dozens of erotic stories all available for one monthly fee…

- **Patreon –** https://patreon.com/kinkywriter

And while you're at it, be sure to also subscribe to our free, email newsletter to ensure that you're the first to know about every new KinkyWriter story!

- **Newsletter –** https://kinkywriter.com/newsletter

Thanks for reading!

KinkyWriter.com – purveyor of fine BDSM and fetish erotica
https://kinkywriter.com